Tales of the Ten Lost Tribes

Tamar Yellin

TALES
of the
TEN LOST TRIBES

The Toby Press

First Edition 2008

The Toby Press LLC
POB 8531, New Milford, CT 06776-8531, USA
& POB 2455, London W1A 5WY, England
www.tobypress.com

© Tamar Yellin 2008

The right of Tamar Yellin to be identified as the author
of this work has been asserted by her in accordance
with the Copyright, Designs & Patents Act 1988.

ISBN 978 1 59264 213 7, *hardcover*

A CIP catalogue record for this title is
available from the British Library

Printed and bound in the United States

To Zoran Živković
writer and friend

Contents

Reuben

Therefore the Lord was very angry with Israel, and removed them out of his sight: there was none left but the tribe of Judah only.

Kings II 17:18

And the king of Assyria did carry away Israel unto Assyria, and put them in Halah and in Habor by the river of Gozan, and in the cities of the Medes.

Kings II 18:11

Whative I was nine years old, my Uncle Esdras came to visit. He was a traveller, and a handsome man. Though short, he had the body of an acrobat, and with his shock of fair hair looked much like my father had in earlier life. Both wore glasses, and both possessed the family characteristics: sobriety, generosity, intellect and bad temper, the wealth of too many talents, and an obsessive nature.

There are birds, the albatross for example, that spend their entire lives in the air. My uncle was like that. He set down only occasionally, and when he did so, it was never for long. His visits were rare and always unexpected, for he was always en route, and the fact that we lay on his route was just a happy accident. He was a bird of passage, and we were his way station.

My father did not share his wanderlust. He was a man of books, an earnest autodidact, whom travelling invariably made ill. He preferred to cover distances on paper, and to read about those faraway places he did not have the stamina to reach. To him there was something faintly reprehensible in Esdras, clicking his heels across the continents.

I still remember the day of his arrival. He wore a pale suit, and carried a small brown valise. This, from the state of its broken corners and the numerous labels pasted onto it, must have travelled with him for many years. He smelt strongly of nicotine, and when he bent down to greet me I was struck by a strange sense of recognition. It would be unfair to say that he was my father made handsome, for my father, too, had once been a handsome man. Truer to say he was my father turned hero: a swashbuckler version bronzed by the desert sun.

My mother must have recognised it also, for her embrace of welcome was a little longer and tighter than was strictly necessary. She had squeezed into her black dress, puffed up her hair, and sprayed herself with the perfume she saved for special occasions. The house was a glade of sunshine and fluttering chintz, and she had set the table with angel cake and flowers.

Into this haven of suburban peace Uncle Esdras entered like a light aircraft, battered and bleached, footsore and world-weary, wanting only an oil change and a wash. But he was not a man to insult hospitality; he had, after all, accepted it the world over. And really it only took a few moments for him to adjust himself. He sat down to tea and promptly turned the table into a map as he proceeded to describe, with cartographic exactness, the route he had lately followed to bring him to us. It was a typical act of conquest. He would never, in all the time he spent there, seem natural in our house, but would become a kind of resident anomaly, like the bizarre carving he had brought us from Africa, which sat on the mantelpiece next to the eight-day clock.

Later I found he had taken over my room, and turned it, in a few moves, into his own, a sort of explorer's base hut. Strange objects were scattered among my childish possessions, dark, worn, heavy things, whose presence made everything else unfamiliar: a pair of thick boots, a leather-covered camera, a canvas knapsack fastened with giant buckles. I did not see how they could all have emerged from that one modest suitcase, but my uncle, along with his many other talents, was an expert and indefatigable packer.

On the bedside table a black sticky volume was lying, bound round with an ancient elastic band and decorated with stains and squashed mosquitoes: my uncle's travel journal. I opened it. It was written in purple ink, in a strange spidery code. Here and there it was splashed with a crude drawing: a temple, a tree, a tremulous smoking mountain.

I do not know, to this day, what precisely it was my uncle did. I thought of him then as a kind of scholar-adventurer, performing in actuality what my father only read about in books: leaping crevasses, discovering hidden cities, recording the dialects of distant clans. I imagined him living a life more dangerous and romantic than that of anyone else I had ever met.

He did not take much notice of me at first. Apparently he valued his privacy, for as soon as he entered the room I was dismissed with a clap of the hands. Later I peeped in to find him lying back on the bed with his boots on, blowing smoke meditatively at the ceiling. This struck me as entirely an adventurer's thing to do.

Afterwards I found that by standing on a flowerpot beneath the window I could satisfactorily spy on him, although there wasn't much to see. However restless his lifestyle, he had the capacity to lie still for long periods. His expression was neither troubled nor entirely peaceful: from the depth of the grooves on his forehead he seemed to be calculating the solution to a particularly difficult sum.

I managed to sit quietly through dinner while my parents and uncle talked, but found it impossible to follow the conversation studded with foreign and exotic words. During dessert I nodded off to sleep, and was ignominiously sent to bed. Three hours later I was up again: creeping down in my pyjamas, I found them, like mountaineers in a tent, playing kitchen-roulette on the tablecloth. My uncle had set up a circle of condiments, my father with skill and dexterity spun the knife; my mother had got out an heirloom bottle of brandy. The stakes, it seemed, were more spiritual than monetary. They all smoked cigarettes, and I felt I had stumbled on something adult, sinister and exclusive, an intimate threesome where I was an unwanted fourth.

This was my first introduction to Uncle Esdras. Next morning I discovered him, a dawn riser, sitting in the lounge with his inevitable cigarette and a line of curious objects ranged on the coffee table in front of him. He did not glance at me, but raised a finger. I stopped at a deferential distance of about three feet and looked at the objects. There was a ball of patterned metal, a fragment of red coral and a string of beads. A tooth, a gourd, a coin, and what I knew later to be a lemur's foot.

Uncle Esdras contemplated this booty, and while wielding his cigarette in one hand, adjusted their positions relative to one another as though playing an odd kind of solitaire. There seemed to be great deliberation in the way he did this, and if I had known better I would have said he was trying to pique my interest.

After a while, having arranged them to his satisfaction, he sat back with a sigh, and finally deigned to turn his eyes on me. I suppose you would like to take a closer look, he said, and patting the cushion, invited me to sit down next to him. I hesitated at first. There was something of the predator in Esdras which I instinctively recognised, but I let my curiosity get the better of me and slid in beside him onto the green sofa.

Then he proceeded to explain the origins of his seven objects. He asked me if I knew the meaning of the word *talisman*. Each of these was a kind of talisman and very necessary to the traveller. The coin, for instance, which was decorated with a curly script, if kept in a pocket guaranteed you would always have two coins to rub together. He had found it by chance in an Arabian market. The coral he had won from an old sailor in Calcutta, who in turn had obtained it from a great fakir. It had the power of calming bad weather when thrown into the sea.

As he described their powers and provenance he threw me quick glances every so often, as if to check whether I believed his tales. My expression must have been suitably wonderstruck, for he continued to tell even more fantastic stories. The gourd, for example, was a magical source of water which had saved his life once when crossing the Sahara. The tooth had mystical healing properties.

I picked up the coffee-coloured beads which hung limply on a dirty piece of string. Uncle Esdras frowned.

Oh, they are just worry beads, he said.

I would have liked to have them for my father, who worried a great deal; but all my acquisitiveness, which Uncle Esdras had so successfully stimulated, seemed hopeless in the face of such valuable items. I laid the beads down and extended my lower lip.

You may handle them if you wish, Uncle Esdras said with formality, and feeling obliged, I rolled the ball of metal embossed with symbols which, apparently, brought its possessor genuine good luck. Of course, he continued, they are only useful to the person who rightfully owns them. If you were to steal that, for instance, it wouldn't work for you.

Indignantly, I denied any such intention. I put down the charm, and one by one he plopped the items into a canvas bag, including, last of all, the lemur's foot, which I had longed but didn't dare to touch, and for which he had still provided no explanation.

And what about that? I asked, pointing.

That, he answered, is a lemur's foot. If you throw it down on the ground when you are lost, its toes will point you in the right direction.

Of course, a compass might have done the same; but this tool dealt in destiny rather than magnetism, and I watched him place it in the bag with envy.

After that, Uncle Esdras ignored me again. At breakfast he spoke to my mother and forgot my presence. When we went for a walk he strolled arm-in-arm with her and indulged in a tensely murmured conversation. Skipping close, I caught a few mysterious fragments.

But why not? my mother purred into his ear. You should settle down. Waiting for you somewhere is a nice woman—

Later I went up to him, where he sat reading the newspaper on the patio.

Those talismans, I said. Do you often use them?

Now and then, he answered.

I thought for a moment. I asked: And a traveller—someone who wanted to be a traveller. Would they need to have talismans like those?

Esdras replied that they were more or less essential. Seeing my crestfallen look, he modified this by saying that they were certainly a great help.

I wandered off, and resorting to my room (which at the moment hardly seemed to be mine), spent the afternoon going through a certain drawer, which my mother habitually referred to as my 'mess drawer,' but which to me was full of irreplaceable treasures. There was my school badge for good conduct, the peacock feather my father had given me and a war-scarred, tournament-winning bouncy ball. A plastic ruby which had fallen out of a piece of cheap costume jewellery and a glass drop from a vanished chandelier. Every one of these objects carried for me a kind of magical and irrational power, quite out of proportion to their actual value; the ball, for example, I regarded as almost human. They had been endowed with the significance which belongs only to children's playthings and ritual artefacts.

As I sorted through them I wondered if I could convince Uncle Esdras of their special qualities. But I doubted whether I would succeed in persuading him to exchange even one of them for a genuine talisman.

*

Of the three main family traits—short sight, a bad stomach and an anxious temperament—my father had more than his fair measure. It was not surprising that he should take refuge in an increasing bibliomania.

For as long as I could remember he had enclosed himself, evening after evening, in his small windowless study lined with tottering books: rabbinic treatises, kabbalistic novels, anthropological surveys of the Jewish nose; histories of seventy generations, lists of innumerable dead. Here, surrounded by wreaths of his own breath (he believed in cold), he would study the art of biblical numerology, trace his ancestry to the house of Solomon or follow the spurious trail of the ten lost tribes. Or, turning the pages of an enormous picture book, he would sate himself with images: with one hundred and one representations of Jerusalem. Jerusalem in woodcuts, Jerusalem in gilt with glittering minarets, Jerusalem as a chessboard with the temple in the middle; mosaic maps, archaeological plans, mediaeval diagrams with Jerusalem as the navel of the world, the world peeled and quartered like an orange with Jerusalem at its centre.

In his youth he had dreamed of becoming an engineer. His first ambition had been to design bridges. He filled his sketchbooks with flying arcs of steel, all of them unviable and unstable, hanging perilously in empty air. He had a supernatural affinity with numbers, and no idea what he might do with it.

Instead he went into business, worked himself to exhaustion and left his other ambitions to lie and rust. Time slipped through his fingers. He knew he should have done something exceptional in the world, and at his worst moments, could at least comfort himself with that knowledge.

Sometimes on an evening I would sit with him and, perched on his skinny knee, turn the pages of some enigmatic text: a poem in gothic script, a plan of the universe embellished with dragons. He would tell me stories of the ten lost tribes, who were carried away and shut up beyond the Sambatyon, a river of rocks and stones which flowed six days and was peaceful on the Sabbath; of the Black Jews of Malabar and their red Pentateuch; of the Jews of Yemen, who refused to return until the Messiah came. For this they were cursed, and their messiah, when he did come, was a disappointment. He challenged the king to chop off his head and watch him rise again; and the king did, and he didn't.

As I grew older I would read aloud while my father sat, his eyes closed, smoking an endless chain of Consulates; and while my father played a game of chess with himself in which neither side ever seemed to win, I would browse through fantastic chronicles of how the Children of Israel were led by Moses through the wilderness of Russia, across the Red Sea at the Bering Strait, and down to the promised land of America.

I asked my father once why he never spoke about my Uncle Esdras. There was nothing to be said, my father replied, placing a hand to his forehead, as though the very mention of it gave him a headache. The brothers had not been close for many years. Esdras never wrote or telephoned. Long ago they had quarreled, but that was unimportant: the crust had long since cooled on that altercation. Most of all, my father was disappointed. Esdras could have done anything: whatever he turned his hand to, he would have excelled. Yet he became nothing; became this wanderer, this will-o'-the-wisp, this drifter. A man of wasted talents and broken dreams.

Now I had seen my uncle, I could not prevent myself from making comparisons: my father the businessman, Esdras the adventurer; Esdras tanned and dynamic, my father sedentary and pale. I could not understand my father's hostility, and thought his reserve must stem from some deep-seated jealousy of his more youthful and enterprising brother.

I thought I detected, too, a certain disdain in my uncle's attitude. He spoke to my father with one corner of his mouth always cynically turned up, and never, I noticed, looked him in the eye. While my father was out at work he went into his room and sat on the corner of his desk, finished his chess game and flicked through his precious books, with the half-smile of one who had no need of them. Yet communication between the two cannot have been entirely frozen, given that once, when I came home from school, I caught sight of them closeted together in the study, and my father, with an air of profound gloom, handing a significant envelope to his brother.

For my part, I was dazzled by the romance of my Uncle Esdras, which was made all the more tantalizing by his habit of ignoring me for long periods, and only speaking to me when he chose. He took up his place in our house with the suave negligence of a visiting dignitary, and was waited on hand and foot by my mother, with whom he held urgent, whispered conversations behind the kitchen door.

It took me a little while, therefore, to pluck up sufficient courage and present him with my first proposal: the exchange of his worry beads for my champion ball, plus the accumulated savings in my piggy bank. I had chosen the worry beads for our first transaction, not because they were what I most wanted, but because I thought that of all the talismans in the bag, they were probably of the least value. In any event, I didn't think Uncle Esdras was likely to need them much. He was cutting his toenails in the bedroom at the time; at first I thought he was going to say nothing, but then to my surprise he laid the scissors down and handed me the cuttings on a small piece of paper. Throw these in the stove for me, will you, he said. And don't drop any. You'd be surprised what a witch can get up to with your toenails. I did as he asked, and returned. Well then, he said, let me have a look at this ball. I brought it out, and we proceeded to go into detail about its tournament record.

To this day I cannot fathom the motivations of my Uncle Esdras: whether he was moved by spite or mischievousness or pure casual greed, or, as seems likely, by a combination of all three, he took up my offer and pocketed both ball and cash. There is, of course, another possibility: that he really believed in the value of his talismans, and only took what he considered fair payment.

As a result of this successful first deal I was both heartened and dismayed. Heartened because the other items now looked attainable; dismayed because I had already parted with all my money. I had a lot to learn, I realised, on the subject of bargaining.

I went off to regroup my strategies, and this required some considerable thought, because I saw that if I was to make the most of my remaining assets I would need to invest them with greater properties than they really had. I did not feel this would be lying exactly. It was more a kind of psychic discovery. By concentrating hard enough I would discover the true powers of these seemingly worthless objects.

So it was that I found myself presenting the plastic jewel for inspection as the seed of a great treasure, which, if planted in a certain spot in China, would produce in due time an actual treasure tree. The jewels, I explained, grew as stones inside the fruit. Uncle Esdras examined it carefully and threw me a curious look, half-sceptical and half-impressed, raising one eyebrow and turning up the corner of his mouth. He wondered what he would do with a treasure tree, and speculated that it might be more of a liability than a benefit. And then, perhaps he didn't have any plans to go to China. He was a difficult customer, but I was ready to fight back. I said it would be a terrible waste not to go to China, and think of all the good he could do with the money; and if the tree were a nuisance he could always chop it down. We argued like this for a while, but the final result was that he took the jewel and I got the lucky charm in exchange for it.

I could see that this game of swaps was going to be hard work, not least because Uncle Esdras was such a moody chap. There were times when he refused to acknowledge my existence, and others when he positively snarled at me. I learned to recognise the signs, however. We were entangled now in a peculiar conspiracy, and when the moment was right he was as eager as I to negotiate.

It wasn't all business though. My uncle had other things to teach me, too. Lying on his back under the moon (since for nine weeks he had not slept in a bed, his body gave him no choice at first but to sleep in the garden), he taught me the names of the stars and the constellations, and described, in his detailed, National Geographic manner, the nights he had passed under a desert sky. He recalled nights in the mountains with stars as big as snowflakes, and low tropical moons the colour of brass. He invoked the cry of the jackal and the song of the bulbul, the call of the cicada and the howl of the wolf.

Why did he travel so much? He started out as a species of shady salesman; invested his money, spent nothing, had no home of his own: not one chair leg, he liked to say with a smile. This was how he afforded his airline tickets, and an endless succession of rooms in cheap hotels. More and more he had gone for the gypsy life, joining a series of ill-planned expeditions: crossing the desert with a flotsam of outcasts, climbing mountains on the bootstraps of lunatics and dragging through jungles in the wake of gangsters. For years now he had preferred to travel alone, and showed no mercy to tagalongs and companions.

It was easy for him to undergo privations. Nothing clung to him: even his clothes were borrowed. He described his sufferings with obvious pleasure, and showed off his forearm, ripped by an angry scar. Every few minutes his face contracted with pain. Sciatica, he told me, adding, with a wry smile, that pain, too, was a kind of companionship.

I begged him to tell me more stories, and he obliged with tall ones: how he had sailed by raft down the Orinoco and visited the Bermuda Triangle. How he had survived snakebite and caught malaria, and escaped an erupting volcano by the skin of his teeth. He told his tales always with a twinkle in his eye, as though silently acknowledging their spuriousness. But I longed to believe him, and while I did so, I think he even believed himself.

I asked him once if he had ever encountered any of the ten lost tribes. He paused and drew breath, as though about to spin another yarn. Then he frowned, and seemed to change his mind.

There was an old junk seller he had met, once, in the backstreets of Shanghai, who claimed to belong to the missing tribe of Reuben, and who had tried to sell him some ancient biblical parchments. But he hadn't been taken in: the man was a charlatan.

The story was obviously true; and this seemed an appropriate moment for us to engage in a little business transaction of our own. I reached into a pocket for my latest offering: one of the onyx eggs from the mantelpiece. It wasn't, strictly speaking, mine to exchange, but I was beyond caring about such minor details. I told him it was the egg of a phoenix. I wanted the lemur's foot desperately, and so far nothing I could offer would persuade my uncle to part with it.

*

Night after night, my father and mother and uncle played the knife game in a welter of cigarette smoke and brandy and an increasingly portentous atmosphere. I would come down to find them gathered round the table, watching the knife spin with the faces of hardened gamblers.

My mother would be gazing at my Uncle Esdras. My father would be gazing at my mother. Esdras, calm and detached, spun the knife with the deftness of long practice. As the blade turned, the mood intensified, so that when it finally slowed and came to rest, it seemed to point with prophetic significance.

And then, one night: You spin it, said Esdras, pulling me onto his knee; and as he did so my father's head jerked up, like a horse's does when it senses danger. For the stakes were now immeasurably higher. His eyes met those of his brother; my mother observed them both; all three watched my small hand spin the knife. Quickly at first, then slower, the blade flashed round. It was as though my whole future depended on it.

My father said to him: It's not your place.

My uncle replied: It isn't your place either.

You've no business to interfere, my father said.

None of us can prevent it, my uncle answered.

Then the knife slowed down, and came to a halt, and pointed at neither my uncle nor my father. It pointed away, through a gap in the condiments: out of the circle, into the distance; nowhere.

*

What did my uncle do on his long wanderings? He looked at the landscape. He gazed at and examined the faces of people. He listened to language, traffic, music, banter. He smelled rot and incense; he tried all sorts of food. He slept under rocks and on benches, in trains and in boats, his cheek against granite, metal, sawdust, velvet.

It was, all in all, an intensely physical life. A life in which thought was consumed by practical matters, and long hours of travel by uninterrupted thought. A life of consulting maps and haggling for tickets, of planning the next destination and bartering clothes; of riding the dragon of the imagination all across Asia.

At least, said my uncle Esdras, his eyes on the stars, that was the way it appeared to him just now. Just now, with his eyes on the stars and his body in stasis, the friendly pain of sciatica streaking his leg, he really believed his travels to be romantic. It was an illusion, of course, and one he fell victim to every time he resolved to end his journey.

I'll let you into a secret, my uncle said. This time I'd really decided to call it a day. But I knew as soon as I got here that that was impossible. Why? I asked him. Well, he said vaguely, I'd already bought my ticket. And he held up an airline ticket against the moon.

Then Esdras told me the truth about his existence. How life was reduced to the merely physical. How slow and tedious were the long void hours of travel. How cold the nights spent sleeping under the heavens. How sordid the far-flung places of the world.

The truth of it is, I am shattered, said Uncle Esdras, and turned on me a pair of exhausted eyes. At that moment I felt a strange presentiment. He turned his face away and looked at the sky.

That was the price of freedom, said my uncle: always to be counting the miles from nowhere; always to travel hopefully, never to arrive. Never to go home, never to be at peace. But he was depressed just now, he immediately added. Whenever he stopped he got into this mood. As soon as he moved on he would feel better. That was why he never lingered long.

You see, he explained, fixing his gaze on the stars (and I wondered how he could see them without his glasses): my mother and father thought he was always unhappy. But when he visited them, he always was.

*

Night after night my uncle spun the knife; and as it went round it wound a spring tighter and tighter inside my father, tighter and tighter inside my uncle too, so that one night as I lay in bed I heard a glass break and my father shouting. Then my mother's voice, querulous and distressed. The deep, impassive tones of my Uncle Esdras.

This time I didn't dare to venture downstairs.

Next morning I found him seated as usual, his bag packed and waiting in the hall; phlegmatic as ever, he turned the pages of the newspaper with a leisurely air. My mother was red-eyed in the kitchen. My father, of course, was nowhere to be seen.

Uncle Esdras was leaving as suddenly as he had come, and I still had not bargained successfully for the lemur's foot.

Nor had I begun to broach the possibility of my coming with him, if not this time, then when I was old enough. We simply hadn't had the opportunity to discuss it. But he was sour and distant this morning, and shook out the paper violently when I approached; so I went off in desperation to hunt through the contents of my mother's dressing table.

His taxi was coming at twelve, and while my mother packed sandwiches and my father sat dourly among his books, Uncle Esdras paced the garden and I made my last reckless offer. Fortunately he was in a mood to negotiate. He wore a sardonic smile; I wondered whether to trust him. But it was his ability to play seriously which was at once so disconcerting and so irresistible.

Transaction completed, he smiled and ruffled my hair. Poor kid, he said. Looks like you're going to take after your worthless uncle.

It was the best compliment I had ever had. We walked down the driveway together, hand in hand. And there was an aura then about Uncle Esdras: a radiance of utter happiness. He had the ecstatic air of a man beginning, all over again, the great undiscovered adventure of his life.

As my mother and I saw him off at the gate (I with a handshake, she with an epic embrace) I felt a sudden pang, not only of disappointment at being left behind, but of guilt at sending him into the world so bare, so unprotected and without talismans: with only a false jewel, a badge for good conduct, a peacock's feather and a bouncy ball.

Returning indoors, I took out my frustrations on my father, who listened incredulously while I told him it was all his fault, that I was going to the Sahara with Uncle Esdras, that I loved Uncle Esdras more than I did him. Slowly, with a pained face, he rose to his feet.

He's a bum! he shouted, and the word sounded all the uglier flying from his unaccustomed mouth. He's never even been to the Sahara. Don't you know he only came here to borrow money?

It was a lie and I said so, running off then to shut myself in my room. My room was tidy, and bore no trace of Uncle Esdras, whose sheets, even, my mother had hastened to remove. It was as though he had never visited. And yet it was not. The dawn of some unpleasant change was breaking in me. For the rest of that day I valiantly held it off, while my mother hunted and inquired after her diamond ring. But after all, I told myself, she didn't realise that it could summon a genie. A fair exchange is no robbery, I told myself over and over, as I rearranged my seven talismans, and ran my acquisitive fingers along the knuckles of the lemur's foot.

Simeon

As for the fate of the ten lost tribes of Israel, it remains a matter of speculation until this day. There are some who hold that they were absorbed and assimilated by the Assyrians among whom they were exiled. Others maintain the belief that they escaped and were scattered throughout the world, living in obscurity until the time of the Ingathering. Certainly, their descendants must exist somewhere, though whether or not as Jews, is one of the unanswerable questions of history.

Kugelmann, *An Anthropology of the Jews*

Some would have the praise of finding out America, to be due to the Carthaginians, others to the Phoenicians, or the Canaanites; others to the Indians, or people of China; others to them of Norway, others to the inhabitants of the Atlantick islands, others to the Tartarians, others to the ten Tribes. But I having curiously examined what ever hath been writ upon this subject doe finde no opinion more probable, nor agreeable to reason, than that of our Montezinus, who saith, that the first inhabitants of America, were the ten Tribes of the Israelites, whom the Tartarians conquered, and drove away; who after that (as God would have it) hid themselves behind the Mountains Cordillerae.

Manasseh ben Israel, *The Hope of Israel*

We were on a white ship crossing the Mediterranean; we did not know where we were; infinite wastes of water lay all around us. For weeks we had pursued a disastrous journey. We had been unhappy in Paris and Zurich, unhappy in Venice; my father had crossed Greece with his head in his hands. In Athens he ate a poisoned cuttlefish. On the third night he took us down to the port of Piraeus, and there, with his body purged and his mind empty, he looked out across the black mucilaginous sea. It was his Nebo. He knew he would never enter the promised land.

The man at the shipping office was sympathetic. A vacation was no vacation if one was ill. One wanted to be home again, pure and simple. For himself, he always spent his vacations at home.

Home is where the heart is, he told us proudly, placing a fist against his ample chest. His office was bare however, a tornado-struck mass of papers covered in dust. Above a shelf of ancient ledgers was pinned a faded map of the Greek shipping lanes, and in one corner a monkey hung in a cage, of which it shook the bars every so often. We were introduced to it: its name was Jacques (it was a French monkey) and it pulled my father's glasses into the cage and broke them.

We booked passage with the Adriatic Line, dormitory class, which, the man told us, though cheap, was perfectly comfortable. Then, impressed by his native friendliness, my mother persuaded me to sing for him.

We were due to sail at seven P.M., and when we got down to the dock around five, there was the enormous dirty-white ship with a large crowd of vehicles and people waiting to board it. We waited with them until about a quarter to seven, when a rumour arrived: the ship was now full and would sail without us. We all climbed onto the gangplank.

After we had been standing there for about half an hour we saw someone we recognised. It was our shipping official, wearing a uniform jacket over his pyjamas. He looked like a man just stepping out of a dream. Our protest had dragged him from his couch of slumbers. He affected not to recognise us at first, but was quickly defeated by his better nature. He looked at us with reproach, as though personally injured by our stubborn refusal to be left behind.

You should not have done this. This is not necessary, he chided my mother, whom he evidently took as ringmistress of the whole affair. Ah, but it is necessary, my mother replied. You must come down from the gangplank, he demanded. But then, my mother said, you will sail without us. For you I will make an exception, he assured her. You and your family are a special case. The truth is, he added confidentially, the whole thing is a terrible mistake. They should have put the cars for Trieste on first. Well, let them do that, then! my mother exclaimed. He spread his hands. But then there would be no room for the cars for Brindisi!

We won't accept special treatment, my mother stated. And without releasing my hand, she climbed to the head of the gangplank.

The official gazed after us mournfully; he had good reason to regret having heard me sing. Meanwhile the clock ticked on. The captain of the vessel appeared among us, distinguished by a cap the same colour as his ship, and assured us that if we would only descend from the gangplank our cars would be safely stowed on the first-class deck. He asked, as a mark of trust, that we give up our passports to him. Many did so, moved by fatigue or by his plausible manner.

But no sooner had we dispersed than the ship's engines started up. Doors were pulled shut and open deck rails closed. We all rushed onto the gangplank once again.

It was now almost midnight, and the captain himself was weary of the standoff. There was nothing left for him but to keep his word, and with great bitterness to load the remaining cars on the first-class deck. This would deprive the first-class passengers of their promenade, but by now nobody cared about them. The crane was recalled. For a few vertiginous moments I saw our white Cortina swinging unforgettably against the night sky, and at 1 A.M. we finally departed.

A steward directed us to our accommodation. For ten minutes we pursued him down a maze of throbbing corridors, until at last he opened one of the heavy, high-silled doors and the chugging engines burst full upon us. We had reached the very bowels of the ship. In half-light, beneath a vaulting of thickly riveted girders, various passengers were making themselves comfortable for the night. Women were undressing behind a makeshift screen. A large man in a string vest and underdrawers was sitting contemplatively on a near bunk with a child across his knee. Apart from the thump of the engines there was a murmurous quiet. Many were already fast asleep.

The steward showed us to our numbered bunks. Here we discovered that not even bedding was provided. But by this time my mother was already dumb with horror. The nearest light bulb had burnt out and one of the bunks was hanging from a broken chain. When the steward gestured to the beds with an expression of complacency my mother burst out laughing.

This can't be serious, she said. You surely cannot expect us to sleep down here.

The steward plainly did; a look of annoyance came into his face. He may not have understood my mother's exact words, but he understood the laughter, and seemed inclined to take it as a personal affront.

Dormitory, he repeated, gesturing to the beds, and in another instant he would have turned on his heel; but then my mother noticed the damaged chain. Just one moment! she managed to detain him. And how do you expect us to sleep in a broken bunk?

This was a nuisance. He tried to mend it on the spot; it wouldn't mend so easily, it was well and truly severed. Meanwhile my father and I shifted from foot to foot. I was beyond exhaustion, and would happily have laid my head down anywhere. My mother, however, was not to be put off. She demanded that we be provided with alternative accommodation. She would not keep a dog in this place. It might be all right for these people (she indicated the man in the string vest) but not for us.

Here my father mentioned, in a murmur, that he did not mind sleeping there himself. This disconcerted her for a moment, but she soon realised that a woman and child alone had more appeal than an entire family. She agreed, therefore, to leave him in the hold, and without undressing, or even removing his shoes, he climbed wearily into the bottom bunk and lay there motionless, with one arm laid across his face, in the attitude of a lost soul.

The two of us followed our steward back into the upper regions, where he led us wordlessly to the third-class lounge and there abandoned us, on the mistaken understanding that he was gone to arrange us a cabin. My mother waited with rising irritation, clutching her overnight bag. The adventures of the evening had put her on her mettle, and she had no desire to sleep whatsoever. I, meanwhile, passed out quickly on the settee, and despite the bright lights and noise, slept like a lamb.

Eventually a young steward with a headful of brown curls and the mild eyes of a doe stumbled upon us and asked if he could be of assistance. My mother told him we had nowhere to sleep. We had been waiting half an hour to be taken to our cabin, but the steward who was looking after us had disappeared. Our young man asked her for the cabin number. Well, the truth was that we had none; but we had been informed that one could be arranged. The doe-eyed man was sorry: there was not a single cabin available, every one was full. Surely we had not come on board without accommodation? He seemed gentle and sympathetic, and my mother confessed the truth of our predicament. If all else failed, she added, we would sleep in the car. We could not be more uncomfortable there than in the so-called dormitory.

The steward regretted to say that to sleep in the car was absolutely forbidden on account of safety regulations. But since our situation was so desperate he would see what he could do. He then vanished. We did not expect him to reappear, but within five minutes he returned with blankets, and seemed to indicate that, on his head be it, we would sleep right here in the lounge.

It was a tender moment. My mother thanked him in several languages; she told him he was an angel of mercy. He smiled in self-deprecation and shook his head. We made ourselves cosy, he dimmed the lights and wished us a comfortable night. Ten minutes later we were both asleep, rising and falling on a rapid sea.

The *Apollonia*—that was the name of our ship—was an elderly vessel, flayed by sun and water, patchily repaired and ready to rest her bones in some tropical breaker's yard, but our crew had not done with her yet. They, like the ship itself, were hanging on till the last click, attired in cosmetic uniforms which covered up a wealth of inefficiencies, but, like the ship's paintwork, were a tad shabby; it occurred to me that they wore the uniforms in order to trust themselves, and also, of course, in order that the passengers might trust them.

That was the flimsy contract under which we travelled. Since it had already been torn up by the shenanigans of the previous night, we felt no compunction on waking next morning in the third-class lounge to find the incurious eyes of the first officer gazing at us. We could not sleep here, he said. But we already had, indeed, replied my mother as she rose like Aphrodite from her couch, we could not sleep anywhere else. At which the officer, knowing the contract was hopelessly in pieces, informed us that breakfast was ready in the dining saloon.

The fact was announced by a tune played on the ship's intercom. We descended woozily. Down here there were no windows and very little air, and a few passengers were picking listlessly at a buffet of hard rolls and reconstituted juice. My mother, her hair standing on end like a weird headdress, drank a cup of very strong black coffee and with a stern gaze, dared anyone to pass judgment on her appearance.

After breakfast I went up on deck, where I was dazzled by an expanse of dirty white against a backdrop of glimmering blue. Everything was cold and hard and bright. A frill of fast foam ran alongside the ship; aft, I discovered a deep swimming pool full of nothing but air.

That day we passed Rhodes, and found that the gate between the third-class and the first-class decks was locked, necessitating a roundabout journey of five or ten minutes to reach our car. The captain, to whom my mother appealed, would not compromise. We third-class passengers could not be allowed direct access to the first-class deck. My mother was disgusted. In her heart she was always first class, and demanded her privileges as of right. But the captain of the *Apollonia* remained immovable.

So my mother picked up her overnight case and led me without blenching to the first-class lounge, which was upholstered in swirls of maroon, and was by no means luxurious, though it appeared so after our view of steerage. Here a bored and child-hating barman reluctantly served us Coca-Cola in the traditional bottles.

We set up camp within sight of our car, and before long I had made the acquaintance of a pretty, dark-haired girl in dungarees called Alex who was on her way to America and who knew everything, including the name of our doe-eyed crewmember, Nikos.

Nikos, she insisted, would fill the swimming pool for us and had only to be persuaded. In fact, she had done a great deal of persuading already. The moment she saw him pass the window she ran out, and with American boldness caught him by the hand. O Nikos, Nikos, she panted, fill the swimming pool for us, fill the swimming pool! I hung back shyly as I watched him, with his patient, gentle look, smile down at her, explaining that the swimming pool was being painted and could not be filled this voyage.

We made it our business to watch out for him. When the tune played for dinner we found him standing in the stuffy dining room, a napkin over his arm, before one of the mock-oak pillars. We tormented ourselves throughout the tedious meal by trying to catch his eye. Later we saw him at the far end of the promenade and ran towards him, but Alex had to stop halfway. I'm not supposed to run, she panted. I've got a hole in my heart. She added casually: I'll probably die before I reach eighteen.

I was stabbed by a pang of envy.

That night my mother and I waited for the surly barman to lower his shutters and depart, then bedded down in the first-class lounge with blankets and pillows, as if in our own private suite. It was Nikos who came to check on us, reacting with nothing more than a wry smile to our arrangements; in fact he carried an extra pillow under his arm. It was in his nature to be courteous and obliging. He sat down on the sofa's edge and talked with us for a quarter of an hour. His manner was deferential but friendly, warm but reserved; my mother, with all her curiosity, found out nothing about him. He answered her questions with a smile and a blush. The sea was his home, or rather, a succession of ships whose duties and facilities were all more or less similar. The perpetual back and forth of endless voyages was all he needed in the way of progress.

The next morning Alex and I spent trailing up and down the promenade decks, teasing Nikos whenever he crossed our path. He seemed distracted, but never failed to flash his brilliant smile at us. We demanded Cokes and more Cokes of the sullen barman. Alex told me they would soon be discontinuing the fluted bottles and that in a few years they would be worth a fortune. I secreted one in my suitcase, feeling like a thief.

In the afternoon she was ordered to take a siesta; I found my father on the second-class deck, attempting to read. The shipboard wind snatched at the pages of his book. He looked more unhappy than I had ever seen him, a man completely at odds with his situation. Where is your mother, he asked, in the melancholy tone of one who has been abandoned. The last time I had seen her she was engaged in fierce argument with the captain, but I did not tell my father so. Nor did he wait for an answer, but turned his glazed eyes out to sea with an expression of desolation.

Before dinner we noticed the strange phenomenon of the sun setting in the east. We were sailing out of the red of a blushing sunset.

Some of us gathered on the rear deck to watch it. It is a miracle, we said. We have boarded a magical vessel. Not since the beginning of the world has such a thing been witnessed.

Down on the promenade I found my mother walking arm in arm with the fat captain. Evidently they had settled their differences, for as they parted he lavishly kissed her hand; a cynical half-smile played about her lips. As soon as I joined her she told me, with some excitement, that we were not going to Brindisi. The island we had glimpsed a little earlier, which some had claimed to be Sicily, was merely Crete, whose northern edge we had brushed and left behind. We were now circling the blue heart of the Mediterranean.

The story told her in confidence went like this: a sister ship of the *Apollonia* had sunk in a recent storm off the coast of Spain; there were not enough lifeboats on board, and other safety features were said to be lacking. It was the second such incident in the past three years. The company was being held to account, an inquiry was underway and all the ships in the line were to be impounded. It was therefore impossible to stop at Brindisi, and doubly impossible to return to Greece. We must bide our time; the fuss would perhaps blow over, but meanwhile, the captain affirmed with tears in his eyes, he would do all in his power to give us a pleasant voyage. Would my parents do him the honour of dining tonight in his cabin?

My mother graciously accepted.

He's a born liar, she concluded, but I think the story is true. Go and fetch your father. I went and found him still sitting out on deck, half-frozen in the cold floodlights, letting the wind turn the pages of his book.

She dressed him in the brown jacket brought for special occasions and herself in the black evening dress she had fished from the back of the car, and together they sailed off to the captain's cabin, leaving me under the care of Nikos. He played draughts with me at one of the bar tables. His long fingers, gathering up the counters, trembled slightly; his breath smelt of something pleasant and unfamiliar. When he moved his head, the light on the lounge ceiling formed a halo behind it.

You are very quiet, said Nikos. I said, I like to be quiet. Well, he agreed, I also like quiet people. But if you are too quiet no one will get to know you. That is the way I prefer it to be, I answered. He smiled. I know you better already, he said.

That evening the wind grew stronger, and around ten o'clock the first flashes lit the horizon. The stewards went about shutting windows with long poles as the rain lashed down. By midnight the first-class lounge was full of people and the liqueur bottles were rattling on the bar. Thunder boomed; the sky turned violet. We're going to sink, I told Alex, and there aren't enough lifeboats on board. She stared at me in terror, clutching her sickbag.

I did not see why she should be afraid of dying, since she was soon going to do so in any case. In fact I was curious to see how her heart would hold out under the strain. But there is nothing to be afraid of, said Nikos, bending over us. The storm is miles away. Listen, count the distance between the lightning and the thunder. His reassurances were broken by an almost simultaneous flash and crash, but we occupied ourselves in counting, and the distance soon grew greater as Nikos moved among us proffering drinks and comfort, the bright lights of the storm illuminating his face.

That night we slept in wasted heaps on the floor of the first-class lounge, and when we awoke it was to find ourselves still circling in the midst of the Mediterranean, in brilliant sunshine, under a blue unbroken sky. That day, to our joy, they filled the swimming pool, and at the ocean's heart we struggled and swam and shrieked in the jostling water, whose high waves filled us with terror and delight. Afterwards we ran Hamelin-like after Nikos to the first-class bar and demanded Cokes for all from the evil barman, who replied that we were out of Cokes, there were no Cokes left, there were no more Cokes for any children. Nonsense, said Nikos, disappearing, and he came back shouldering a case of bottles which he opened and distributed among us. They were not chilled, but we did not care so long as we had defeated the hated barman. For the rule of children had broken out on the spellbound ship.

From that time we sailed in a zone of enchantment, through blue days, through nights brilliant with stars. Round and round we sailed in our magic circle, until the days ran together, we could not say how many, nor how many still and perfect nights, in which the mesmeric tune for dinner played over and over, the captain broke open his best wine, and the after-dinner entertainments ran on far into the small hours; when music played from the white ship strung with lights over the dark and silent sea, and the captain danced with my mother, my mother danced with Nikos and Alex danced with me.

Nothing was beyond the multitalented Nikos. He soothed my father's restlessness by matching him at chess; he distracted him and made him smile with number puzzles and with long, intense conversations at the ship's rail. He flattered my mother with compliments, and drew the fascination of the children with demonstrations of magic and discourses on the curved nature of space, by virtue of which, he told us, if you travelled in a straight line for eternity, you would surely end up back in the place you started. He was the master of treasure hunts and distributor of sweets, keeper of secrets and healer of arguments. We were under his aegis, a dreaming contented crew. We would have been happy to sail forever with him towards an unreachable horizon.

Seated at the large table in the first-class lounge, he spread for me the map of his aspirations: the Mediterranean which he called the Blue; but also the other seas, the Black and the Red, the Arabian and the Caspian, and the oceans, the Atlantic and the Pacific; the straits and bays, the gulfs and archipelagoes, all the waters he hoped one day to cross.

And this is how I mostly remember him: standing at the rail on the first-class promenade, in one of the idle moments his duties allowed him, gazing out to sea with a solemn expression, though if you were to speak to him his face would be lit, as though inwardly, by a benevolent glow. He was in love with distance, with the horizon pure and simple: the expanses of sea and sky which bored others to annihilation.

How often I watched him, on that voyage which seemed to go on forever, folding blankets with elegant precision, or mending a broken toy a child had dropped, his long brown hands quite certain of their movements, or bending, with just the right degree of intimacy, to hear the request of a seated passenger, nodding with unfeigned interest and concern. How often I saw him smile, and his perfect smile inevitably answered. He had the gift of getting people to talk; I could not resist him indefinitely, and, on a long dull evening of cards in the first-class lounge, he finally charmed me into parting with a few choice secrets I immediately regretted.

That was his fatal flair. He knew everyone and was known by nobody; and so it must have been on countless previous ships.

By the sixth day of the voyage too many hearts had been laid waste on that vessel. Wherever he went he was tagged by begging children. Even my father actively sought him out. My mother made eyes at him over the breakfast rolls. In the privacy of her cabin Alex showed me the small gold ring with which she planned to woo him. I was numb with resentment, and could not bear to speak to her thereafter.

On the night we turned north into the grey finger of the Adriatic, we older children were allowed to stay up for a captain's party in the dining saloon. The glow of those lost days had left us the moment we changed direction; the passengers were full of complaints and anxiety once more. Dinner was a gaudy, drunken affair. Coloured balloons had been pinned to the walls and ceiling, and the stewards stood about with hangdog expressions, knowing that this disastrous voyage would be the *Apollonia*'s last. This time next week they would be washing dishes in some landlocked taverna. In honour of the occasion the captain opened a jeroboam of champagne—no one knew where he kept this lavish stock of vintage—and sang a sentimental folk song, out of tune, through a whistling microphone and without accompaniment. It was absurd, laughable: the ship was herself again. Nevertheless, my mother stood on her chair and proposed a toast to the *Apollonia*, to her captain and crew, and most particularly to Nikos, loved by all. His name rang through the ship with the pathos of hundreds of unrequited passions.

Later he found me on the promenade, gazing at the stars through a blaze of tears. What is the matter? he asked, in that gentlest of voices, but I would not answer his too indulgent question. I could not tell him I wished he and the secrets I had told him were lying at the bottom of the sea. You're jealous of Alex, he said, because she is special. But she's not the only one with a hole in her heart. He looked at me then with a meaningful expression; and I did what I have ever since regretted. I turned my back and walked hastily away.

We sailed on comfortlessly northwards. It was late August, the fag end of the season, and autumn was already in the air. It was too cold to swim: they placed a rope net over the swimming pool. On board the *Apollonia* rations were running out. There was no more juice for breakfast, and a complete and catastrophic absence of gin. We survived on black coffee and bile as far as Zadar, where we were dropped off with the captain's apologies. Some of us promised to sue the shipping line. We embraced each other like the oldest and closest of friends; and then the *Apollonia* hauled anchor and sailed away, perhaps forever, but she must have been eventually impounded. The last glimpse we had of her was of a white ship plunging southwards through the grey waves of the Adriatic, as we made our way up the Dalmatian coast. It may not have been her. It may have been only a vision.

That was the end of our maritime adventure. We returned home, where it was quickly transformed into an anecdote, one of my mother's dinner party pieces, though my father never contributed to the telling. For myself it faded into the blur of childhood, into a vague trail of images and sensations: a dazzle of white, a restless glimmer of blue; a little dark-haired girl with a hole in her heart; a bottle, long since discarded, with a fluted design.

And yet for years we continued to hear from Nikos. A postcard would come, already faded and greasy, depicting some vessel in the Tyrrhenian Line, the *Star of Ionia*, the *Delphi* or the *Heraklion*. He would send his greetings from the ends of the earth, for astonishingly he had not forgotten us. This although we had no way of replying, nor of proving that we had not forgotten him; for he was, I suppose, one of those exceptional people, whom to meet once is to remember always.

The last we received was, I think, from the *Damietta*, a ferry which sank with all hands, under criminal circumstances, shortly after the close of the summer season; but I do not believe that Nikos was still on board. I think he moved further east, to the Indian Ocean, and later on worked the ships of the South China Sea, enslaving hearts in thousands of brief encounters, and meeting his end, if at all, by the blade of some desperate, envious devotee.

We never heard from him again, however; and while I continued to look out for him among the anonymous crews on numerous crossings—his brown curls greying a little, his mild eyes unmistakable—I saw him only in occasional dreams, where, asleep on the soft bed of the Mediterranean, he lay with my childhood secrets locked inside him forever.

Dan

On the third day we set sail, in a boat without nails, through a sea of serpents; and on the seventh day of our voyage we reached an island where dwelt Jews of the tribe of Issachar. These traded in jewels and spices, and in the streams of the island there was much gold. They studied the scriptures and kept the Sabbath, and their king rode upon a leopard ten yards tall. There was no theft or murder among them. They lived in peace and prosperity, until such time as they should be recalled.

Eliezer ben Levi, Travels to the Ten Lost Tribes

It may come as a surprise to discover, on investigating the subject scientifically, that there is no statistical reason for regarding the hooked nose as particular to the Jewish people. As a matter of fact, my investigations among a wide range of Jews have proven just the opposite, and it appears that if any type of nose is to be regarded as typically Jewish, it is the straight, or Greek variety.

Fishberg, The Jewish Nose

There are forty-eight Jerusalems.

Jewish tradition

These were the curious means by which my father pursued his books: there were the book fairs, of course, and also the specialist bookshops, but he did not really feel comfortable in these. There were searching and ordering services, but these were too easy, too impersonal. A modern bookseller's, I think, he hardly set foot in. No: he must haul in a catch of dross to bag a nugget. He must look for books as if he were panning for gold.

From an early age I accompanied him to the auctions, held in large and draughty warehouses, which were the closest he ever came to gambling. There were carved dining tables, standard lamps, boxes stuffed with china and antimacassars, disassembled and mournfully waiting beds. We picked through the ticketed and numbered lots, underlining the 'Miscellaneous Books'; my father studied the catalogue like a primer. Then the auction began. There was crowding and a smell of overcoats. The auctioneer ran his gavel over the bids, the bidders raised their catalogues to his gavel. Patter patter patter and SOLD! to the man in the homburg hat, who was my father.

In this way we acquired the *Midnight Book of Horror, Household Management* and a leather Bible dated 1803. We bore home a soapstone discus thrower and a Roman charioteer who had lost his reins, a set of brass bells, also a stiff and dusty Spanish doll.

My father took pride in this booty, which might be valuable and was dirt cheap; one could always, after all, dispose of the real rubbish. One never did, however. It was always so difficult to judge what rubbish was. Sanctified by a bargain, the charioteer sat on the mantelpiece with his reins of wool: he was regularly dusted, had a new lease of life, and might even believe himself immortal.

As for the books, my father so rarely discovered what he wanted. And yet he was always interested in them. It was as though he must handle all the books in the world, even if he did not actually read them. They must pass through him like sand in an hourglass. Perhaps he retained a grain or two of knowledge; nevertheless, the pursuit was unstoppable.

It was Mr. Shatzenberg who assisted him in his quest, giving him the lowdown on the best auctions, seeking out the next necessary book. Mr. Shatzenberg, whose name my father said meant 'mountain of treasures', kept shop on an island of rough ground near where the gypsies lived, and was himself a sort of traveller: he had never intended to stay where he was for so long. His shop had a grille on the door and a rattling bell, and was filled with the former property of the dead. He had once had a shop just like it somewhere else, and his whole ambition was to have one somewhere better.

Seated in his windowless back room, under cold fluorescent light, beyond the dark labyrinth of haunted furniture, he drank black tea with my father and discussed all the places he would not go because they were not good enough. My father listened with a distant smile, nodded sometimes, occasionally murmured his agreement. The world was a worn-out place, and here was the evidence. All these old and broken things, these exhausted and battered items, waiting patiently to do their duty: it was all too easy to identify with them. I crept, while they talked, through the ever-altering labyrinth, where I was soon engulfed by a maze of sideboards and dressers and tallboys blooming out of the dark. With their smell of spilt ink and dust and mahogany, they resembled the giants of some Amazonian forest in which I had lost myself. I floated downriver on a chaise longue, or set up camp behind the battlements of a leather chesterfield; took shelter under a pedestal desk or climbed the mountain route over a stack of chairs. I frightened myself sometimes with my own sudden image in a mirror, or with the unexpected appearance of a stuffed bear, clutching a hat and stick, whose grotesque smile seemed to mock my pretended adventure. And there were other animals too: a bird in a glass, a screaming sinuous stoat, the head of a deer whose brown eye, full of gentleness and sorrow, seemed to reproach me for the cruelty which had killed it.

All this was magical and terrifying, until the men finished their tea and conversation. Then Mr. Shatzenberg snapped on the single light, and the mystery was extinguished in a moment. A forty-watt bulb shed a dull truth on things: not quite good enough to see details by, in contrast to the brightness by which he drank his tea. Death filled the room, unequivocal and prosaic death, the kind which clears houses, haunts flea markets and sits on bonfires.

Mr. Shatzenberg said: I will do my best on the book, for he was a man with a multitude of connections, some might say, both in this world and the next. If one wanted a certain kind of Persian rug, or a secondhand set of red Bohemian glasses, he could get that too, by way of an unknown source. Nothing was beyond his powers of obtaining. Books he conjured from some secret dimension: a cosmic library, perhaps, of decaying tomes, where not one volume was unavailable.

I saw in my father's eyes a kind of hunger, sharpened now where most it was satisfied, for he never left here without yet another request. As they shook hands I saw the incompatibility between them, my father with his love of cheap shoes and cheap haircuts, Mr. Shatzenberg with his signet ring. Yet as they shook hands they were unmistakably brothers.

We both love a bargain, Mr. Shatzenberg said. That is why we understand each other. And my father smiled dimly, having been diddled again, and thanked him for the black tea laced with strong white sugar, his taste for which, it is true, he shared with nobody else I ever encountered.

My mother disliked Mr. Shatzenberg, to whom she believed

my father was in thrall, and whose powers of salesmanship made her deeply suspicious. She came with us once to the shop, and for almost an hour pretended an interest in an inlaid table for which he was asking an astronomical price. He knew she would never buy it, but bargained with a bitter rectitude matched only by her courteous disdain. She wrinkled her nose at his miserable back room behind its dusty drape of orange velvet. Her disapproval meant we must visit by stealth, always on the way to or from somewhere else, and always for nothing more than a few snatched moments. Perhaps that is why I feared him, felt him a little dangerous to know: a criminal perhaps, a confidence trickster.

But what, after all, did I know about Mr. Shatzenberg, whose entire substance was composed of his business, and whom I never saw or imagined in any other context? He lived alone in the rooms above his shop, whose windows were covered up with dirty curtains, and emerged sometimes from a maze of unseen back rooms, the purpose of which I could only guess at: an endless series of them it seemed to me, stuffed with an endless treasure trove of objects; and beyond them all the secret hidden workshop where Mr. Shatzenberg dropped tiny fragments of marqueterie into place, mended the bindings of his precious books or brushed the dead pelts of his stuffed menagerie.

Yet he did call us up once, on one special occasion, to share a glass of sherry in what he called his apartment. And how strange it was, to mount the forbidden steps, to see the door open on his unvisited lounge: a grand miscellany of ponderous furniture, the walls splashed with brown autumnal flowers. We sat on a carved sofa as hard as a rock and toasted something in ugly crystal glasses; I was allowed the merest, tiniest sip, enough to spread a sweetness over my tongue. Viennese elegance had strayed into a slum: one bulb glowed in the massive chandelier and the windows were draped in faded crimson chenille, but where these items had come from no one remembered. They were displaced remnants, like Mr. Shatzenberg himself; one day they too would be taken down and disposed of.

Yet he drank his sherry with genuine enjoyment, refilled his glass and also topped up my father's, although it was barely touched. He was, after all, a man of enthusiasm, never more so than when he was on the trail of an item. No one could be more sincere in his promises than Mr. Shatzenberg when my father wanted a book, and there was always one—the One—my father wanted, always a cause for conspiracy and pursuit. It was I who must be engaged to take the phone call, delivered in his characteristic voice, clipped and specific, but blown by suppressed excitement: Please will you tell your father I have the Book. And always it seemed that this was the ultimate volume, the one my father had hunted for all his life, the one which would hold the answers to all his questions. But it was never The Book, the final book of books, the mythical grail of books he was pursuing.

Now, from this distance, it is not easy to tell how far my father was motivated by his own desires, and how far by the manipulations of Mr. Shatzenberg, who had probably never read a book in his life, but who fully understood the sensation of hankering after an object just out of sight. He did not fail to notice, for example, my own interest in a certain clear-topped cabinet full of bits of faceted glass and rings and chains, among them a genuine seal for sealing genuine letters, letters fixed with a button of red wax marked with the head of an emperor. But he did not open the cabinet, not the first time or the second or the third. Only the fourth time he saw me looking did he unlock it, offering me fob watches and inkwells and friendship brooches, none of which I wanted, and only then did he consent to bring out the seal, which I touched at last with burning acquisitive fingers, to be told it would cost me an unachievable sum.

So we left the shop, both with the taste of the near miss in our mouths; and my father, I noticed, looked tired, like a man who has been running too long and too far, chasing himself in endless impossible circles. When he reached home he would shut himself in his study, run his hand abstractedly over the shelves, fetch down first one volume and then another. It was as though the prospect of getting his book distracted him from reading anything else. He could not concentrate; his brain was buzzing with a weary excitement.

My mother asked him where he thought he was going to put all these books, since the house was already full to its bursting point. For she was always for clearing out and losing weight, for freeing herself of unnecessary burdens. So my father sorted out some books for disposal, placing them mournfully in a cardboard box. Look, he said, I am getting rid of these. And these. And he threw in some fake Lladró figurines for good measure. Then he took them down to Mr. Shatzenberg's and asked what he considered a generous price. Mr. Shatzenberg peered and smiled like an undertaker. Now really, my good friend, do you think I will be taken in by such tactics? This is not the proper way to do business. (For some of the books were ones he himself had sold him.) But he did not understand that my father was a man entirely without tactics, naked and unarmed in the business world. Or perhaps he did. In any case, the boxful went for a song; my father never ceased to regret its contents.

It was inevitable, for Mr. Shatzenberg's currency was pure desire, and an object's value lay only in its being wanted. His whole graveyard of junk was worthless flesh without spirit, the mere empty vessels of its former owners. The bones themselves could not have been more poignant. Yet he himself was no materialist. He hankered after no objects of his own. I remember him proudly displaying the brand new alarm installed on the crumbling wall of his apartment: gleaming, incongruous, it resembled a giant padlock affixed to nothing, an elaborate fastening on gates of air.

One week's notice, he liked to say, and I can be done with this. The whole kit and caboodle. Less than a week. Three days. You don't believe me? Just give me the chance. You think this stuff looks heavy? Trust me, it's light as a feather. I could vanish, you wouldn't know where I am. I've done it before and I can do it again. My father smiled faintly and looked depressed, and seemed just then to feel himself terribly heavy, weighed down by all the possessions and all the books. Towards the end of his life he always looked laden. His face was that of a man who expects to be crushed.

But Mr. Shatzenberg was burdened with nothing. Even his signet ring was up for sale. He turned his mountains of clutter into money, and money, too, was merely a matter of numbers, weightless numbers floating in the bank. He moved with ease like a dancer among his goods, with the loving elegant gestures of a salesman. How beautiful, his gestures seemed to persuade us. Money is nothing next to beauty like this. Of course I understand your hesitation. But come again next week and it may be gone.

Meanwhile, my father grew to depend on him for a stream of increasingly rare and abstract books: for his genealogies and atlases, his obscure monographs and mediaeval texts, for travel accounts whose bizarre dreamlike descriptions kept him up into the small hours of the night, and what better time was there to read and believe them. He brought them home wrapped in brown paper tied with string, and cut the parcels open almost with trepidation: the first moment of handling was so fleeting, and no subsequent moment was ever as pure. A book once read was used, faded, too intimate to be parted with, too familiar to be read again.

How many interminable hours I sat with him while he worked on that massive compilation, his *Tales of the Ten Lost Tribes*, and while he constructed, bridge by difficult bridge, the hidden network which connects us all. For this was my father's secret undertaking: to trace migrations and reclaim names, to exhume the missing and retrieve the dead; to create a synthesis of all he had read and learned, and set it down at last in some kind of order, a map of the maze in which he had lost himself. He began at first with nervous tentative notes, tall blank sheets with headings, brief unreadable scribbles. The notes flowered and multiplied, put out branches and roots, grew in a papery mass across his study. He worked through the night, categorizing his knowledge into sections and subsections; he left for work in the morning hollow-eyed. He filled up cashbooks and ledgers with his jottings and came home triumphant with the card index which would solve all his problems, but a month later there were three card indexes scattered over his desk and the order he sought had proved as elusive as ever.

Really the work was impossible to finish, for the boundaries of his task were limitless. And then, of course, his memory was failing. His memory could only hold so much. So often when I came across him reading, his finger was pressed to the centre of his forehead, as though to keep in place the precarious knowledge which threatened constantly to fly apart.

I was reluctant now when he asked me to join him, and during the long evenings when I did not dare to slip out of the study, I listened to his muttered self-reproaches while I turned the pages of the gigantic picture book—Judith and Holofernes, the pillar of cloud, Elijah and his fiery chariot—whose red-and-black text was as familiar as my own face and behind which I was able to shelter a little. But I could not avoid my father's disconsolate eyes, or the page of illegible notes he thrust before me, pleading, It does make sense to you, doesn't it? Just a little?

In the back room at Mr. Shatzenberg's shop he dipped Marie biscuits in his tea and discussed business with a strange abstraction, his gaze locked attentively on his hands. He matched the surroundings, had grown a little decrepit, and wore week in, week out the same rusty jacket with its same troubling stain on the lapel. His odd smell made me recoil, but Mr. Shatzenberg did not appear to mind. Nor did he seem disturbed when my father lost his way out of the shop, but calmly touching his elbow, guided him to the door.

Now you take care of your father, the shopkeeper said, and it was I who had to direct him, a man who once learnt route maps off by heart, down the streets of our local neighbourhood. On the way we stopped frequently to examine the various species of lichen on the wall, the different trees, the names on shopfronts, to discuss their origins, and to pick up fragments of litter for possible study. There was nothing in the world which was not evidence, no link too trivial to be pursued.

As I guided him down streets which, because of the sheer intensity of his gaze, he no longer recognised, he walked with the shuffling gait of a traveller whose long and tiring journey was almost over. His back would not straighten, his leaden feet would not lift: the feet of the young man who years ago had tried to leap oceans with his imagination. Each step would take him nearer to the last edge, and each slow step would be followed by another.

But I do not know if he thought he would ever find what he was looking for, or if, in the long hours when he sat in his study, gazing at his chess set covered in dust, he did not lose hope, acknowledge at last the futility of his search. Yet I clearly recall how he emerged one morning, no longer exhausted but radiant and scrubbed, as though from a Turkish bath, with the face of one who remembers not a thing, and fully expects to begin at the beginning.

That was the day we made our last visit to Mr. Shatzenberg, a bright day when I looked at the seal locked in its case of glass and found that the very sight of it sickened me. Desire had finally consumed itself. My father, too, was unusually silent, without his accustomed enquiries and requests. And Mr. Shatzenberg did not seem to notice. His busy enthusiasm was the same. His trade, after all, was quite unstoppable: there was no lack of insatiable clientele. And as for the discus thrower, the Spanish doll, my father's whole library and the charioteer, they would all find their way to some other auction, and burden the sideboards of some other house. My mother would see to that. But Mr. Shatzenberg would remain faithful to my father's search. The day would come at last when he cried with triumph, with an almost irrepressible schoolboy glee, I have The Book! And perhaps he had really found it; but my father could no longer receive it then.

Naphtali

There can be little doubt that some of the Jews living in these isolated mountainous regions trace their ancestry back to the migrations from Mesopotamia, possibly as long ago as the sixth century B.C. Indeed, they have been identified as such by travellers throughout the ages. For centuries they lived in their high auls or villages, forgotten by the world, and it is hardly surprising that until the middle of this century they should have remained more or less undiscovered, concealed as they were amongst a population consisting of eighty-one different peoples speaking thirty-two languages and innumerable dialects.

Kugelmann, *An Anthropology of the Jews*

Neither is there any weight in the Argument which some have brought to me, if they be in the world, why doe we not know them better? There are many things which we know, and yet know not their original; are we not to this day ignorant of the heads of the four Rivers, Nilus, Ganges, Euphrates, and Tegris? also there are many unknown Countreys. Besides, though some live in knowne and neighbour Countreys, yet they are unknown by being behind Mountains; so it happened under the reign of Ferdinand and Isabel, that some Spaniards were found out by accident, at Batueca, belonging to the Duke of Alva, which place is distant but ten miles from Salamanca, and near to Placentia, whither some Spaniards fled, when the Moors possessed Spain, and dwelt there 800 years. If therefore a people could lie hid so long in the middle of Spaine, why may we not say that those are hid, whom God will not have any perfectly to know, before the end of days?

Manasseh ben Israel, *The Hope of Israel*

Why did Moses stammer? Because of the impossibility of translating God's language into human language.

Sages

W hen I left home for the last time it was autumn, and I took a student room with grey walls where I hung my dead mother's picture and came under the aegis of Professor G. Professor G. was my tutor, a man of glacial poise and rigid authority, my new father, from whom I could expect no sympathy. I believe it was his philosophy that the young should be made to suffer, and I was more than ready to oblige.

One of the first things I heard about him was that he had once tried to kill himself. I was surprised he had not succeeded. His body was full of potential violence. I felt that when we sat, for so many hours, in his narrow, sarcophagal study stuffed with books; it was evident in the coiled, averted position from which he held nearly all our tutorials, never or rarely looking me in the eye. From this angle he presented more sharply to view the powerful outline of his Slavonic jaw, where it was distorted by an unnatural lump: a tumour, as I was eventually to discover, not malignant, which he was on a waiting list to have removed, and which bloomed meanwhile beneath a carapace of shiny skin, polished at intervals by his immaculate fingers. He was, despite or even because of this, a handsome man, in rather an ice-blue manner: nearer sixty than fifty years old perhaps, but lithe and muscular, something of a panther, and not in the least complaisant or benign. His accent I never could identify, but then I was no connoisseur of accents. It seemed to me Russian, then Scandinavian; German, too, and sometimes nasally French. His clothes were always stylish and suited him well, but these, I discovered, were not of his personal choosing.

I had heard, and was soon to experience evidence, of his absolute passion for language. A high priest of grammar and brilliant philologist, he was fluent in more than twenty different tongues, and read with comfort in dozens of alphabets; the story went that he liked to dream in Swahili. No one who studied under him could fail to be dazzled by his almost supernatural facility, a gift which, while inspiring to some, was overwhelming to others, in part because of his uncomprehending contempt for those who were not privileged to share it.

They were numerous, and I too was among that number. I remember how dismally I failed at the first hurdle of his stringent testing, when he asked me if I could manage a simple task: to translate the front page of *The Times* into biblical Hebrew. I hesitated, and doubted if I was able. This earned me an attack of acidulous scorn. You should be able, the Professor insisted. If not, you should not be studying under me.

With that he uncoiled himself and turned to the bookcase, and reached for a little black Apocrypha. When he rose I noticed that he towered some six and a half feet over the narrow room. Without turning round he thrust the book towards me, intoning the single, terrible word, Translate! I did so stumblingly, while he looked out of the window, correcting my howlers with spitting theatrical outrage, approving my better efforts with nods of assent. He then sent me away with the instruction: Translate this whenever you've nothing else to work at, and keep on translating until you have finished the book.

Later I would learn how futile it was to attempt to impress him. Yet then I was eager to salvage myself in his eyes. I remember the resolve with which I purchased my only ever copy of *The Times*, sitting down with gusto to work on its pointless and laborious translation. Fortunately the front page news was of war: my biblical lexicon was not too absurdly stretched. I altered names to their ancient equivalents, and here and there, with a touch of impious humour, worked in well-known expressions from the psalms. The news of the day took on a scriptural tint: the hand of God was at work in the world once more. The task, after all, was instructive, and when it was finished I thought myself teasingly clever.

How was I to know that Professor G. would choose just this moment to sink into one of his periodic depressions, and that my precious handiwork, slipped through his box at the Oriental Department (I hadn't the courage to present it in person), would vanish into that black hole of the unmarked in which the work of generations of students had lain for decades? A lost and forgotten heap of their best efforts, of which the melancholy professor remained quite unaware.

But I did not know then how darkness overwhelmed, how silence descended on him from time to time. I did not know how language abandoned him, sealing him in a perfect speechless bubble.

By our next tutorial the professor was not speaking, and it was more than a little disconcerting to address the back of his head for nearly an hour as he stood like a statue with his face to the window, communicating in a series of grunts. I was young and touchy, and thought that my smart-alec effort must have annoyed him. I was mortified that this silence might be its result. I promised myself I would never again try to be clever, a pledge which proved easy enough to keep.

Yet I could not help blaming the zeal of Professor G., for luring me into the flames of his disapproval, or his lofty pedagogic heartlessness, in leaving me there to baste myself with shame. I never quite forgave him this first encounter, despite the fact that he never referred to it, and although I was glad he had never read my translation, I also grew to resent its permanent loss.

From those who knew him better I was to learn the various stages of his depressive illness. In health he was irascible but brilliant, moody, enigmatic, hard to please; a man of mercurial whims and intense opinions, who loved to alienate his closest friends. When melancholy he grew increasingly silent, seemed almost to forget the most common words; was at the same time gentle, tender, wistful; needy, even, of confidence and support. From this condition he generally recovered, returning more or less to his usual self. He might, on the other hand, descend into madness: a violent storm locked tight as an oyster shell.

In time I would come to know him better myself, to recognise the trivial hints and symptoms, the shifting markers of a coming phase, and to take in my stride the unreasonable behaviour which used to drive me to the verge of tears. I learnt to accept his rare approbation with grace, and to swallow his critical comments with quiet poise. I learnt, too, to feel sorry for this man, who returned from his sick leave paler, older, gentler, purged in some way, like one who has been on retreat. He never talked of his illness. It stood between us, the shadow of something appalling, unspeakable.

It was from his wife that I discovered the true secret of Professor G. and the source of his subtle torture, the ironic torture of a man whose whole soul was language. She was his interpreter in the world, an artist of luminous beauty, a woman of profound magnetic calm. It was her hospitality, I had heard it said, which kept the vituperative professor in friends. Her garden parties and dinners were legendary, her cooking alone was an international language, and the frequent artistic and academic gatherings at the professor's house contributed a good deal to his reputation. The house was beautiful, a white and gold floating dream, with tall french windows opening onto the garden: a perfect reflection of the woman herself. There were cool rooms filled with paintings, white furniture, backlit religious artefacts; flower arrangements, trailing jardinieres; a library lined with books from floor to ceiling. It was from this sheer cliff face of books in all their variety—the dark spines of German and Italian, the papery spines of Arabic and Chinese—that one gained one's sense of the professor's astonishing knowledge. And yet it was the unplanned glimpse of his chaotic study—dark brown, unadorned, awash with papers—that truly gave one an insight into his mind.

Led by the serene presence of Mrs. G. through her resplendent house, one could not help drawing contrasts between the two, nor avoid thinking of the professor, hovering like a black danger mark among his guests, as the surly Beast of this enchanted garden. He did his best however, and while his wife served out batches of delectable finger food or cooked up redolent casseroles, he attempted to engage those young scholars with whom he had nothing in common, or those old ones with whom he had little to share except a mutual interest in cuneiform. He spoke always in clear, precise sentences, and listened hard, like one who is perpetually translating in his head. This made him a somewhat formidable person to talk to. If there were foreigners present he never missed the opportunity to converse with them in their own language, even (or especially) at the expense of somebody else. Occasionally he tossed a few words to his wife in French; and once or twice in a language I could not identify.

He was as much a guest as ourselves in the home his wife had created, and which really had nothing whatever to do with him. While he liked to assume the role of the connoisseur—opening bottles of wine which she had selected, pouring them out with a coy unsteady hand—he had, in fact, no grasp of what he was doing. He read the labels with childish puzzlement; a guest asked for red and he filled his glass with white; he did not seem to realise the difference. His clothes, too, so unerringly chosen, hung on his angular body like borrowed robes. He plucked at them nervously sometimes, as though conscious of his uncongenial and anomalous air.

And yet, when roused on a subject he cared about, the professor could bring passion to the gathering. He could talk intensely, even amusingly, and fill the table with gales of delighted laughter. His impersonations were second to none: he had an undoubted talent for being somebody else, and his occasional renditions of foreign poetry had the power to mesmerise even those who knew not a single word of the language.

It was in this context, I remember, that I managed to injure myself against the spines of the great man's arrogance. He had been mentioning Lorca, and I, still eager, even then, to impress, and having drunk half a glass of Pinot Noir, announced my admiration for his plays. This turned the ice-blue eye in my direction for what must have been the first time in several weeks. The professor had not been aware of my knowledge of Spanish, a knowledge I hastened at once

to disavow. I had, of course, only encountered the works in translation. The professor's eye instantly hardened from ice into rock. In
that case, how on earth could I claim to know them? Having thus
flattened me he turned coldly aside.

I was silenced, mortified; I felt the whole party observe my
humiliation. I was wrong, of course, for later I would discover that it
was the professor's rudeness, rather than my own pretension, which
caused the ripple of discomfiture to run round the room. As for
Mrs. G., she rose to the occasion. When an appropriate interval had
elapsed she invited me into the kitchen to help stir the mole; there,
without fuss, she apologised for her husband.

I do not recall exactly how much she told me as, with bejew-
elled fingers, she broke little fragments of chocolate into the shining
pan. Piece by piece, in the period that I knew him, my knowledge
of the professor would fall into place; it is she who in many ways
remains enigmatic, as all beautiful people perhaps are, with her dark
hair pinned in a chignon against her neck, her soft quiet accent, and
her calm eye denying any implication of unhappiness in a marriage
which must at times have been unbearable. She knew something of
my own background, and sympathised with me in the time-honoured
manner of those who avoid their own suffering by focusing on that
of others. I was for my own part cautious, I remember, the recipi-
ent, at that time, from many people, of a kindness I could not trust
because I knew it would not last.

Yet there is little doubt in my mind now, looking back, that
she was genuine. Who knows what she had endured in the way of
prolonged silences, intimate sickness, the pure blubbering anguish
of the professor; his social barbs being only the stray shots left over
from an arsenal reserved mainly for his private life, and aimed for
the most part suicidally at himself. She was the one who had to witness the self-destruction of the man she loved, at the same time as
her own needs were entirely ignored. For this, however, she neither
expected nor invited sympathy.

Of course, as she was well aware, I could not have failed to
know something of the professor's illness, both through my own experience and through gossip. Indeed it is only by a combination of all

three that I am able, now, to retell something of his story. She was not the most forthcoming of sources. Her manner was one of dignified reticence, but our kinship in suffering broke the ice between us, and she told me more, perhaps, than she did most acquaintances.

It is, I suppose, the heart of the story, the soul of it, that she was able to give me. For while others had the facts, the facts themselves were difficult to grasp. They said nothing, they were meaningless; for this reason alone it was impossible for most people to empathise with the professor. They blamed his depression on faults of personality or chemical imbalance, and no doubt these elements also played their part. Without them, perhaps, he might have been almost normal. But the real issue, the cryptic problem of language, was too essential to him to be easily comprehended.

I am conscious of that in describing it myself. There is something in my account of the professor which must go untold, which is quite literally unspeakable. That is the speck of void at the heart of his being: the silent zone into which he sometimes fell, and where we cannot follow without sharing his madness. His wife alone must have known something of it, and what she knew she was not willing to tell.

And yet I cannot help recalling to mind her own predicament, that she was an exile too, obliged to operate in a foreign language: a circumstance always evident in her accent, but to which she hardly ever chose to refer. It was her husband's plight she considered tragic, his loss of that rare, irreplaceable mother tongue, whose distance and absence caused him constant pain. Her own situation she regarded as common, and nothing more than a mild inconvenience.

I do not know if it was on this occasion, or on some subsequent one, that she pointed out to me, on a primitive map which hung outside the professor's study, his landlocked, remote and mountainous place of origin: one of those tribal regions cut off at the best of times, and now almost impossible to access. The name escapes me, and the map must have been unique, for I have never been able to find it on any other. I don't remember the exact circumstances which, out of all his family, brought him here alone, making him the sole native speaker, to his own knowledge, of that language in which his whole identity consisted. For apart from memories he carried no other tangibles of his early life: nothing but language linked him to his former existence.

He had been ambitious in his youth, swept up on the tide of his own hungry intelligence, and it is more than possible he blamed himself for the situation in which he was now trapped. So much the greater his distress, his feeling of fundamental abandonment. His linguistic brilliance had carried him to the pinnacle of his field, but the first foreign words he had ever spoken had been learned not out of desire but out of necessity.

One can only imagine the fierce pride and frustration with which he determined to master that other tongue: a horror of being forever verbally lost which must have resembled, at times, the fear of drowning. Fear fuelled him, vanity drove him on, compelled him to master language after language, to do so down to the patter, down to the slang. A cast-iron rigour belied his apparent facility: his idioms were acquired at terrible cost. It was his driven wish to be a foreigner nowhere which gave him his mixed unidentifiable accent, an accent which marked him a stranger wherever he went.

No doubt his own triumphant struggle had leached him of sympathy for that of others, leaving a pitilessness which most of his students had felt. His apprehension of the nature of language was heightened by his predicament, so that there was a real sense in which he considered it untranslatable. Hence his impatience with neophytes like myself, who ignorantly claimed to have studied Lorca.

His wife had first met him in Paris seventeen years ago. She encountered, as she later described it to me, a man existing on a rarefied intellectual plane, a person almost impossible to relate to. Only later did she discover that these so-called rarefied matters of intellect were rooted in her husband's very guts. The word for love existed in many languages, but only in his was it derived from the word for anxiety. There was a complicated cultural reason for this, which he explained to her at length over their first dinner.

At this time, she soon learned to her horror, as well as engaging in a punishing academic schedule, he was maintaining his embattled grasp of his—by now—long-since redundant mother tongue, in the only way he was able: by carrying on nightly dialogues with himself. Of this she might have remained quite unaware, had she not stood at the door of his room one evening, waiting to knock, transfixed by the sound of an incomprehensible and one-sided conversation. In order to convince her of his sanity he was obliged to explain his desperate measures, which included writing long letters to his family (which, of course, he was unable to send), a private diary, a variety of academic essays (which, as he freely admitted, could never be published) and, really for his own pleasure, the compilation of a grammatical diction-ary. He hoped that one day his labours would prove useful, but in truth they were no more than a valiant expression of his struggle to hold on to, retain, clutch, just keep alive the few vanishing strands of his native language. For what would be left inside if he let them escape him? A terrible, an unimagined silence.

For Mrs. G., the revelation of this heroic secret pushed aside all questions of sanity. She was benevolent by nature, always eager to help: she understood the anxiety of love. It would be much better for him, she reasoned, to have a partner in his efforts, someone to whom he could teach the fundamentals. She was not entirely untal-ented in language, already having learnt the use of two. In time he would have a fluent speaker to talk with, someone to read his by now voluminous writings, a partner not only in body but in mind.

The auguries were not good. Shortly before their wedding he wrote her a letter in French—it must have been well on in our acquaintance that she told me this—in which he advised her to marry somebody else. He would never want children, he warned her, because 'he could not bear to imagine them looking out at him from behind their foreign eyes.' That, at least, was how she interpreted the phrase. He might have been referring merely to their 'strange eyes.' Whatever he meant, she chose to ignore the letter. Exactly three weeks later they were married.

She held him to his promise and became his student, though he now evinced a curious reluctance to teach her, born, she thought, of his conviction that he was bound to fail. For his was, apparently, a language of nuance: a web of associations gave it its flavour, and these she could never hope to grasp. She gained the essentials, she understood the grammar; they even conversed sometimes, on mundane matters, or when they required a moment of secrecy. But her well-meant attempts to talk on a deeper level reduced her husband to inarticulate rage. They only served to endorse his isolation, and confirm his sense of being essentially mute.

In the early days, she told me, she had been puzzled by his impatience to abandon their lessons, surprised, even, by this apparent apathy in a man so driven. Later she had wondered whether he really wanted to share his language, whether he did not prefer to keep it to himself. It was, after all, the source of his uniqueness, the paradox which made him what he was.

And if this was true, if he did so wish to protect it, the fact she must have come to realise was this: that it was far too late now to rescue her husband. Nothing she could do would change his fate. She saw how he was spiralling into silence, in a chain of effects she was powerless to break.

That, she told me, was when I began painting more than ever. I was trying somehow to paint the silence, she said. We were sitting at tea in her immaculate lounge; a summer breeze disturbed the long white curtains. All around us her silent paintings hung: white also, numb, and painfully void, in a room resembling a lovely necropolis.

I remember the scene particularly, because that was the last time I saw her at that period. In fact it seemed her only appropriate setting: a beautiful, chill and anaesthetising cloud. Shortly after, I took my examinations. Like so many others before me I went on my way. For a long time I hardly thought of the professor. His strange predicament faded from my mind. He and his story were forever associated with a time which was painful and which I preferred to forget. And then, years later, in a foreign cafe, while locked in a private reverie of my own, a hand touched my shoulder, a soft voice uttered my name. It was Mrs. G. herself, the professor's wife, and yet I confess I barely recognised her. She laughed as she had to remind me who she was. She was changed, older, more lined, with streaks of grey in her hair; and at the same time younger, more colourful, more flamboyant. She wore a long robe splashed with oriental patterns. She was alone;

she invited herself to my table. She sat there vibrant with laughter and gleaming with rings. She asked me how long I had been living here. I explained that I was only passing through. What a fantastic coincidence! she marvelled. She had a studio overlooking the river, a nice little place with flowers and plenty of light. I would have to come over and see it: she wanted to show me her paintings. I would probably die of shock when I saw them. No more white pictures, she told me, that was all past. Her work had sprung to life when she discovered colour.

That was when she told me about the professor. His second suicide attempt, she said, had not been unexpected. For years his deterioration had been evident to everyone, and since his retirement the long periods of almost total silence had been punctuated by only a few bouts of increasingly feverish talk. Drugs had reduced him at last to complete dumbness. By this time, said Mrs. G., she had not been able to communicate with him at all. She could not describe the wretchedness of their life. She had abandoned her painting, for the simple reason, as she confessed with a smile, that she had nothing whatever to say. As for the professor, he no longer read or wrote. He sat, merely. A few words were sufficient to reduce him to tears of grief or rage.

How could she put into words the sheer misery of it, the isolation? The doctors diagnosed him with a depression. Nothing she said could make them understand. They were well-meaning, of course. But after the suicide attempt, when he was accounted as better, they expected her to continue as before. She couldn't do it. It was beyond endurance. Finally she had decided to bring him here. There was an excellent sanatorium, twenty miles away. Once a fortnight she drove out there to see him. Meanwhile, after a spell of loneliness, she had set herself up in this little studio. In time she had even started working again. She had found friends; she was no longer alone. For the first time in many years (she admitted to it with almost a guilty smile), she really believed she regarded herself as happy.

She looked down shyly then, and appeared to concentrate on the scrap of paper she was neatly folding over in her hands. Of course, she went on, if it was solely a case of her own happiness, she could not wholeheartedly consider it as such. But—I would hardly believe it—the strangest thing had occurred at the sanatorium. The staff had informed her of it a fortnight ago. It seemed that, of all the places in the world, it was here that her husband had finally met the one person he had always needed. It was truly remarkable, the nurse had said, but since his arrival he and this man had never stopped conversing. They talked on the terrace all day; they talked at mealtimes; it was all the staff could do at night to persuade them to retire to bed. It was hard to believe that the professor had had the good fortune at last to run into another native speaker; but as for his wife, she was only too glad to offer up her personal prayer of thanks.

It was her chief source of comfort to know that, while she was selfishly embarking on a new life, her husband, too, had found some consolation. And she did not wish any crude doubts to intrude on her joy just yet. The nurse had said it was strange, but the inmate in question had for years been accounted a speaker of nothing but meaningless gibberish; and here it was found to be all the time a sophisticated language. True, they had listened for hours and understood not a word of what passed for communication between the two men. But then, most foreign languages appeared that way; and even gibberish must have its own intricate and peculiar grammar.

Gad

Scarcely a people on earth but has been identified by someone with the missing Israelites. The Kareens of Burmah were said to have a 'Jewish appearance.' The Hindus of Kashmir possessed a 'Jewish cast of face.' The Basques, the Spanish, the Franks and the Huns, the Creoles, the Mexicans, the Afghans and the Japanese, all have been at some time or other located as one of the ten lost tribes.

Kugelmann, *An Anthropology of the Jews*

When we had passed through that place we travelled thirteen days in the desert, until we reached the kingdom of the Danites, which is at the edge of the wilderness. To the north of them is the country of the red men, and to the south is a great sea. They ride horses, but they eat no flesh; they possess the Torah, Prophets and Writings. In their kingdom are many trees, the fruit of which is strange. Their synagogue stands at the centre of their city; they pray there every day for the Redemption, and its ark faces west, towards Jerusalem.

Eliezer ben Levi, *Travels to the Ten Lost Tribes*

When she was very young she had left home with the intention of finding her freedom. She planned to catch a boat and sail abroad. She had never got farther than the port, however. That was more than forty years ago.

Now she still lived in this remote northern port, whose very name was a byword with runaways, and where the ships put out daily for the wider world from a harbour whose tangle of tarred rope and rotting timber attracted her from the first. She had found work in the customs office, and took note of the shipments leaving and entering the country—grain paper, hanks of cotton, lead—while she remained exactly where she was, year after year, forever poised on the cusp of her intention.

She claimed to dislike the port, which was grim, unlovely, full of drinking men, and which contained nothing of beauty except a hard brick church, whose tower was a landmark for those returning to harbour, and whose colourful east window depicting Jonah and the whale commemorated the innumerable lost. And yet she remained there. For twenty-seven years she had lived in the same small flat at the top of a tall house high above the town, a place of almost conventual simplicity, whose windows faced north towards the open sea.

She had never married; and her family were unable to understand why she stayed alone in a place where, by her own account, she was not happy. For their part they would not have dreamed of living in the north, far less of leaving the country altogether. They were perfectly contented where they were. But she had always been the rebel among them. She had had to assert her difference. Now it was obvious that her rebellion had not brought her satisfaction. They were gratified in recognising the fact. But the more they tried to argue and persuade her that she would be better off returning home, the more obstinately she refused to entertain the prospect.

It was a point of contention when she made her regular visits to the south, as she did on festivals and holidays, travelling down on the old railway which served the port: a line which, like the port itself, was declining in importance, and was becoming badly in need of renovation, its antique rolling stock now more picturesque than swift. In the early days it seemed obvious to her family that she must return, and they felt no inhibition in saying as much. Later, when it was clear she would not soon do so, they continued to speak of it as a certain fact. Now, after all these years, they were resigned to her staying, but still referred to it as an aberration, a youthful mistake which, God willing, would one day be corrected.

All this irritated her terribly, not least because she felt the truth of it. All that was scathingly said of the north was true. The north was cold; the south was temperate. The north was remote; the south was easy to reach. The north was a cultural wasteland; the south was refined. The north was provincial; the south cosmopolitan. The food in the north was impoverished and unhealthy, though her family gobbled up with alacrity the strong smoked fish she brought as a special treat.

Yet she would not let these arguments influence her, and stood out steadfastly at first in favour of northern merits: for the grit and energy of the local people, their straight talk and blackish sense of humour, for their doggedness in times of adversity and their proud maintenance of old traditions. She soon gave up defending them, however, because while she did admire these qualities, she could not help feeling, in her heart of hearts, that their grit and doggedness were a little brutal, their straight talk sometimes offensive and their traditions mired in ignorant bigotry. They had not opened their fortress gates to her. She remained, after all this time, a stranger among them, and while it may have been partially her own fault (though really, to be fair, she couldn't help it), after thirty years she was still a southerner.

No hint of this ever passed her lips when she was at home, yet her family seemed to know it in any case. You'll never be one of them, sweetling, her mother would say. It was the diminutive title of affection which made her determined never to agree. And yet she was lonely, lonely. How desperately she longed for the journey south, how eagerly she watched the landscape change as the tedious train chugged its weary way. With each softening of the skyline, with the almost imperceptible greening of the fields, she knew she was drawing closer, and the long dull ache of the elastic knotted under her heart, the length of springy elastic which kept on pulling her home, relaxed at last for the space of a few hours. There was the same old house she had grown up in, the same old rooms; her own bedroom unchanged with its sprigged wallpaper. They ate off the familiar china and her mother always cooked her favourite foods; they sat at table in their usual places. There was an air of festival in her homecoming. As the years wore on she still looked forward to those reunions, to the rambling garden now running with nieces and nephews, for whom she was an exotic visiting aunt. Then there were deaths, naturally, and funerals; births and weddings; the loss of the family home; the carefully gauged, more formal invitations to the houses of her various relatives. Her brothers and sisters were always happy to see her, and yet she knew that at heart they pitied her: the now aging and eccentric aunt, returning from her eyrie in the north, dowdily dressed, her face hardened by weather, nursing the blade of her terrible loneliness.

And as for her, the return was not so simple. No sooner had she settled in her room than a smothering sense of oppression overcame her. Home was no more than a prison with patterned walls, a cage hung with fatally beautiful flowers. She longed to pack up, to go away again. She thought of the north, of refreshing ocean breezes, of her desk at the window looking out to sea. She knew that that was her true place of belonging, the only place she really wished to be.

So for the length of her stay she would be possessed by a strange restlessness, an all too evident eagerness to be gone. She remembered, as if it were yesterday, the sensations which had first compelled her to leave, and which now, in bizarre and inexorable repetition, compelled her to leave home all over again.

For it seemed to her now that while the north was natural, the south was pretentious; that the north was a wild place and the south was tame. The north was a dangerous edge, the south landlocked; the north held promise, the south was a dead end.

But there was something else more sinister happening, a sense that she had drawn near once again to a whirlpool of irresistible sucking power: the terrifying and annihilating force of the family, which she must immediately and at all costs evade.

Now it was with the same eagerness that, at the end of her visit, she boarded the train again and watched the slowly transforming landscape, noting the gradual darkening of the hills, the sudden appearance of a rocky outcrop, the very perceptible chilling of the air; the houses becoming meaner, the farms more sparse; the first, heart-expanding glimpse of sea. She hardly knew why it was that the journey filled her with such anticipation, as though something wonderful were awaiting her, nor what it was she really expected to discover, on reaching the port again and finding it just the same, completely unchanged after her few days' absence. The feeling did not leave her as she mounted the tall steps which took her to the top of the town, and even as she flew upstairs to her door. Only when she entered the bare, slightly damp apartment, which seemed to have turned a bit shabbier while she was gone, was she suddenly seized by a terrible depression, a child's powerless longing to be home.

Of course, the intensity of the feeling did not last, and when she had pulled herself together and made a cup of tea, sorted her dull mail and set about her business, she was once again the same as she ever was: hardworking and efficient, a creature of routine, not unfriendly but rather turned in on herself, living with a thrifty self-denial. Which is not to say she did not have her moments of self-indulgence too, but by and large she was back on an even keel; not happy, maybe, but enduring a low-level and bearable measure of unhappiness, to which she was so accustomed she hardly noticed it. Home was a place for which she felt nostalgia, the ache of a dull tugging under her heart, the sort of melancholy which gave her pleasure. She smiled repeatedly over the same memories, and lived in anticipation of her next visit.

Perhaps she did not fully realise the paradox, the clash of contraries at the heart of her life, as she sat by her window gazing at the horizon beyond which freedom still waited to be found: a horizon which, so common knowledge taught her, could never in actuality be reached. And yet it was that sea, both a barrier and a bridge to her aspirations, which had drawn her all this way, which still drew her, on the full length of elastic which allowed her as far as the port and no farther, to tantalise with all its undiscovered possibilities.

She would think then, even though she was getting older, that one day she would really board that mythical boat; and a truly ecstatic moment would run through her, especially at night, when the white lips of the waves crawled towards the shore and the distant lights of vessels winked out of an insubstantial darkness. But perhaps this was the one true, the only actual moment of freedom. For a minute later she would be seized by mundanities again: by money questions, and the fear of strangers, and wondering where she really meant to go; and would she even know a word of the language? And almost at the same time she fell victim to a strong desire to drag herself back home, weakly and abjectly to admit defeat: to throw herself back into the maw of the family, whose triumph, as she well knew, was the most crushing and destructive there could be.

But she never allowed herself to give in to these impulses. And although her overwhelming sense of failure—failure to go on, failure to return—filled her with despair, she knew that the last thing she wanted was for others to see it. She swallowed the despair, she kept it hidden; it sat inside her like a bullet of lead. Perhaps it was the slow seep of that poison which gave her her grey, pale look, remarked on even by the people of the port, who observed her wandering the cliff tops alone at evening and thought her strange, a solitary woman who always had a wan smile for you but never had much to say. They thought it was because she was an outsider, a southerner, a snob, probably, who thought herself better than them. They could not understand why she had come here. They, too, could not understand why she chose to stay.

She could not deny that she took a certain pleasure in playing the part of the town character; that she deliberately walked the cliffs to give them something to point at, and especially in her later years, when she was living on a small pension, dressed eccentrically and picked up a habit of singing to herself. She let them think that these were southern characteristics, that that was the way everybody was down south, and she exaggerated her southern accent, in the same way as, when she went home, she liked to adopt a broad coastal brogue. The people at home were equally gullible. They thought the way she behaved was pure north; and it was for her almost a matter of personal pride, to be a southerner in the port and a northerner in the south, even while she knew herself to be neither.

The truth of the matter, which she often contemplated as she sat at her bare window, was perplexing: that to be neither was to be, effectively, nothing; to be a stranger for the rest of her life. And she thought once that this must have been all she had ever really wanted, a perverse wish, unwittingly fulfilled.

The thought scared her. She wondered if there was time to undo what she had done. That summer, her favourite niece came on the train to visit her, the first time any of the family had ventured to the port. She determined to make her welcome, to show her the attractions of the north. With schoolgirl nervousness she greeted her at the station, led her too lightheartedly up the hill: this young woman whose upbringing had somehow prepared her to take control with great confidence of her own life, and whose admiration for her she had always feared to be unfounded. Now she was to encounter the sordid truth: the narrow, dank staircase to the battered door, the dingy flat with its unpainted walls and a few wild flowers as its only adornment; the creaking divan on which she would have to sleep, and the plumbing which banged like ghosts through the floors of the tall house. It was appalling. She was full of apologies. The niece seemed shocked, but said it would be fine. Later she took her on a tour of the town: down to the rat-infested harbour, to the shabby lighthouse and the drinking dens, past the prefabricated office where she worked, up the steep, stinking alleyway to the cliffs. From here one looked down on a view which, it had to be admitted, was not edifying: the town itself gained little in the way of romance, and the sea walls fortifying the coast were ugly. Only the sea itself, dotted as it was with a few cargo vessels, retained anything of that beauty she had often boasted of. She saw the place now through her niece's eyes, and was mortified. Even the weather was a disappointment. Her whole life seemed to be written in the contours of the landscape, she saw it for the first time as it really was: rotten, squalid, baulked, provincial, empty.

It didn't matter that her niece pretended to be charmed. At the end of a week she went back by train to a nice life in the south, where she was soon to attend the university. It seemed unlikely she would visit again. Nor did her aunt wish her to. As soon as the train had pulled out of the station, she put on her madwoman's hat and went for a long walk. It was lashing with rain, and she must have cut a suitably fantastic figure. She walked close to the edge. It seemed to her symbolic to do so, for she recognised her existence now as a gigantic trap: one of her own creating, that much was certain, but one which was nevertheless impossible to escape; and she laughed at the irony of it, for escape had always been what she most wanted. It occurred to her then that all life was a trap of one kind or another, and she came as close as she had ever done to jumping over the cliff: an act she had never seriously contemplated before, and which she was too much of a coward, she decided, to go through with now. She went back to her apartment and ate cake instead.

That was the situation in which she found herself. And it was the situation in which she remained, however many years later, when she and I encountered each other on the northbound train, that same superannuated train which dragged itself, panting, to the brink of the ocean twice a day, only to turn and run down south like a frightened animal. It was even older now, arthritic and creaking, fraught with a dozen worrying squeaks and noises. Time and again it threatened to jump the line, but one knew it would not, that it would stick to it forever, held on course by inflexible iron rods. And there was, after all, something safe and endearing about the shabby carriages furnished in yellow wood, the leather seats which in hot weather smelt like a rodeo saddle and the antique mirror hanging on the wall. She sat very still beneath a faded advertisement for a funicular railway, and when I struggled with the stiff window, she opened it for me with well-practised hands. I asked her if she was going to the port, a stupid question, for, as she replied with a slightly sardonic smile, neither of us had much choice in the matter. I must have looked sheepish, for she then asked, more kindly, and by way of a joke, if I was headed for the port myself. I told her I had a ticket for the night ferry.

I will never quite know why she decided to confide in me, and in me alone, so far as I am aware, the foregoing story of her whole life; a story, as she readily admitted, completely devoid of incident or excitement, or even a measure of tragedy or romance, though she did feel, in a vague way, that there might be a moral in it somewhere. But that was for others to judge. She was in a remarkably good mood, and carried a shopping bag heaped full of southern delicacies, which she was very eager to share with me. We ate like gannets, and she told me about herself, with a fair quantity of grim laughter; indeed, she seemed just now to find the whole thing funny. But she had strange, black, unreadable eyes. I was rather sorry to have drawn their attention, when I told her I was leaving the country for good, and that I was an orphan, without family connections of any kind, and that this small case held all my worldly possessions.

A moment later she smiled again, however; she touched me on the hand and wished me luck. At the same time she brushed away a tear, but kept smiling as she admitted she was jealous. She could not help seeing in me something of herself as she had once been, setting out with all her aspirations; and she warned me not to follow her example, but to get on that boat without a backward glance. I asked her why she didn't do the same, adding, with the arrogance of youth, that it was never too late, there was always time to change.

She laughed again, and said it was ridiculous, but she was afraid of water. The very thought of sailing made her sick. She had been on a boat once, many years ago, and had almost vomited over the side. The sea was very beautiful to look at, but the idea of floating above all those cold fathoms filled her with terror; which was why the sea had been to her, always, a symbol of both the possibility and the impossibility of escape.

She had always preferred the train, she said comfortably, settling back against the stained morocco; and she loved this line in particular, for all its faults: the view from the window, the way the landscape passed, the sense that one was really going somewhere; the smell of the carriage, the rhythm of sound and sway. She had made the journey more times than she could remember, it must have been literally hundreds. In this train, more than anywhere, she felt at home. It was ironic, perhaps, that she, who had always thought of herself as a natural traveller, was in reality no more than a time-hardened back-and-forther; but after all it was what she relished most. One was always filled with delicious anticipation, on the way south as much as on the journey north. It was, indeed, only arriving which disappointed. Travelling itself was always a joy.

I agreed with her; and for a long while we sat together in silence, gazing at the countryside flashing by. I did not dare mention what I felt she must surely know, that the line, like the ferry itself, was under threat, that bureaucrats were conspiring for its closure; and I could not imagine how she would survive the loss of what was in the most essential manner her lifeline, the axis along which her whole existence was built. And then, I thought further, looking into her face, which was lined with age and wore an expression of serene enjoyment, how would she live, where would she die, where would she be buried? I wondered if these questions troubled her, or if she had at last passed beyond all these tiring unanswerable questions, to a mere acceptance of everything she was.

But we were drawing near to the station; we both drew breath at the first sliver of sea. She gathered up the debris of our picnic. I anxiously dragged down my small valise. You look nervous! she said. I admitted that I was. It was the first time I had gone abroad alone.

Please don't be, she said. You must be brave, you know. It was then that she told me what she had not described before, her own first arrival at the port. How when she first left home it had been with her heart in her mouth, against her most primordial impulses, while all her instincts had begged her to remain; how when she reached the port with a ticket for the night ferry she had been consumed with misery; how she had gone down to the harbour to look at her boat, the *Helena*, and how, in the sheer agony of terror, she had watched it sail slowly from the dock without her and disappear into the evening sky.

You mustn't let that happen to you, she concluded. Heaven forbid that you should end up like me. And she smiled once more, as with an eccentric hand, she caressed my hair and looked into my eyes, no less intensely than if I were her own offspring, whom she was dispatching with all her love and concern into the world.

She turned away then and walked across the platform, and that was the last glimpse I had of her. I made my way down to the dock and secured my place on the ferry. No doubt, later that evening, she watched it sail away from her high window, murmured a *bon voyage* perhaps, and wished, with a pang, for the hundred thousandth time, that she had had the courage to be aboard. But before long she would be travelling south again on the train, which was the one place where she was happy. So it would continue until the service ended. But when she returned north for the last time she would be facing forwards, as she had told me she always did, to feel the impulsive power of the train, and to keep it flying with the full force of her ardour out towards the horizon.

Asher

The retroussé, or snub nose, is more commonly found among Jews than most people might think. According to my researches, some twenty-two per cent of Jews and thirteen per cent of Jewesses possess this type of nose. It is generally considered quite attractive, and, by some, the appellation 'saucy' or 'cute' is often applied to it.

Fishberg, *The Jewish Nose*

Since it is obvious to anyone that the ten tribes still exist, and since, despite all kinds of adversity and persecution, those of Judah and Benjamin now number many millions, one may only speculate as to their vast hordes, their physical strength, and spiritual prowess, having lived secretly scattered throughout the world, without suffering any such persecution.

Rev. John Austen, *Secrets of the Tribes*

And it shall come to pass in that day, that the Lord shall set his hand again the second time to recover the remnant of his people, which shall be left, from Assyria, and from Egypt, and from Pathros, and from Cush, and from Elam, and from Shinar, and from Hamath, and from the islands of the sea.

Isaiah 11:11

Within three days of my arrival I had found a room, on the fourth floor of this decayed tenement block, on Simon Peter Street, in the old tanning district. It was one of those buildings missed by both bombs and the demolition ball, which still stood intact while all around its neighbours were having their guts removed, in the cynical way now popular with town planners: their fragile frontages propped up by matchsticks of scaffolding against the empty air. It had a facade of tall solemn women and art nouveau flowers, and had probably been beautiful and exclusive once, but now its days of elegance were over; until some property magnate chose to renovate, it remained a cheap means of living close to the heart of the city.

The landlady, a sharp, shrunken woman wrapped in bombazine, seemed suspicious of me at first. A large sum of money up front, which I thought extortionate but which I was later assured was usual, helped to set her mind at rest, and she contented herself with watching my comings and goings from the small grilled window of her boudoir on the ground floor. I had the privilege of watching her too, or at least her kitchen, across the inner courtyard from my hallway. She rarely appeared there, but a maid, dressed in traditional black-and-white uniform, spent hours preparing vast quantities of food, I could not imagine for whom: it seemed enough to feed an army of old ladies.

My place lay at the top of eight flights of dim steps, whose cleanliness declined with each floor, and whose only daylight came through a grimy dome of glass high above. On closer inspection I found this to be a once beautiful confection of green and red and blue panels, their patterns now obliterated by dirt. The bannister, too, was a trelliswork of leaves and flowers, broken off in places and covered in dust. My top floor apartment was probably not as grand as the lower rooms, but it still bore evidence of more stately times, in the tall windows, the classical architraves, and the traces of stencilling below the cornices.

The mistress of the house, who soon changed her mind and decided just as arbitrarily that she liked me, explained that the property had been put up by her father, in the days when this was a fashionable part of town; that she had lived nearly her whole life in the apartment on the ground floor, had married and raised a family there, had seen the area and tenantry decline, and remained there now alone, enlivened only by the visits of her grandson, an expensively suited, beautiful young man, and his brood of children, for whom, apparently, she provided those mountains of elaborate food. The fortunes of the district mirrored her own. She had, like the building, an air of faded glamour, and in her ripped lace carried herself like one of the fallen aristocracy.

I quickly learned to take account of her foibles, a skill essential to a quiet life. It was necessary to acknowledge her face at the window, with a dignified nod, every time I passed; to allow her to look over my shoulder at my mail, whenever I came down to collect it from the box in the hall, and never to indicate any feeling of impatience or hurry if she chose to detain me in conversation. Questions about my personal life, or about my fellow tenants, must be negotiated with a diplomat's finesse: she always had a distinct purpose in asking them, and would not be fobbed off with obvious evasions. In return, I received from her information which I did not always wish to be privy to; knowing that she would discuss me with the other residents with just as little discretion and fully as much relish as she discussed them with me.

As things fell out at first, I did not see a great deal of them. A face passed me on the stairs occasionally, or a hunched overcoat; and sometimes, in the dead hours after lunch, the sound of a violin rose mournfully from several floors below. I would pause to listen to it while I studied or prepared lessons. But clearly my habits did not fall in with those of the other occupants. I often went out late, when evening was already falling, and wandered the streets of the city as it grew dark: stumbling on hidden alleyways and sudden squares, and emerging time and again on the edge of the river, the broad, grey, doomy, phlegmatic river which cut through town like an emblem of history. There was in these labyrinthine lanes with their abrupt glimpses of life something which drew me on, always the stranger and observer, as if in pursuit of some discovery: some extraordinary building, perhaps, crouching among the others like a cat, or the luminous face of a child as she looked up momentarily from her play; snatches of music or argument, occasional laughter, bits of existence in which I had no part. As night thickened I would head inevitably for the brightly lit bridge where people gathered in summer, and where the oblivious crowds milled back and forth above the stream of black water; and where sometimes I would meet and talk to those I knew. Many nights I was drawn off by the lights and music to the resurrected quarters of the city, striding there in the wake of energetic companions whose sole ambition was to drink and dance: pursuing that buzz of lights and jungle of music which had settled over the city like a cloud, a bright, precocious, evanescent cloud hovering over its gloomy monuments.

More often than not I would delay the return to the silent darkness of my room by a late visit to the Simon Peter Bar, just along from my aristocratic building. Like many such places it did not advertise its presence, and some weeks passed before I first noticed it. A modest sign indicated its establishment in seventeen eighty-two, but nothing was left of the original hostelry. It was as plain as a five-and-dime store, brightly lit, full of red banquettes and melamine, and at one in the morning it served a decent cup of coffee. A few desiccated sandwiches sat under a plastic dome, and if one was really desperate one could order a plate of french fries, but its greatest advantage was that one could sit there for as long as one liked without feeling under an obligation to order more or move on. It was, inevitably, popular with a regular coterie of lonely and sleepless people.

The proprietor, a man of very few words, seemed to bear these regulars no grudge, supported as he was by a dour, large-bicepped assistant. One in particular, I noticed, an elderly man of untidy appearance, would sit a good hour in front of a glass of mineral water, reading the newspaper with minute attention, and not his own newspaper, moreover, but that provided by the establishment, which he would at the end of his session carry away, for all the world as if it was his by right. I often watched him, his tangled silvery head bent above the broadsheet, turning the pages carefully one by one and occasionally, with magisterial deliberation, picking his nose. He read as though he made a study of it, as though not one word should escape his most particular scrutiny: a man pursuing the clues of a holy scripture.

The Simon Peter Bar, once discovered, became my salon. There can be something addictive in such places, especially when one has nowhere very comfortable to retreat to. Before long I was going there every day, and so, I soon found, did the newspaper man. I never saw where he appeared from or where he went, but the fact remained that he was always there, already seated in his usual place, or, if I arrived unexpectedly early, creeping in soon afterwards; never acknowledging the silent proprietor, who wiped the table hastily and set down his glass, from which he took two or three sips at the most before departing. Sometimes I glanced up from my book to find that he had vanished, and only the glass remained; sometimes I dragged myself wearily off to bed and left him still tracing the hieroglyphs of the late edition.

It happened on one occasion, around two in the morning, that we left simultaneously. No sooner had I paid my bill and risen, than he stood up likewise, packed his paper into an untidy bundle, and pulled on his deeply unappetizing coat. I glanced in his direction: he was absorbed in tying his broken belt, which held his distended form together in the same way as a piece of string might bind a bundle of hay. Our eyes did not meet, and immediately after I left I heard him follow.

It was a dark night, and at this hour, either through municipal penny-pinching or as a result of some oversight, Simon Peter Street was not lit. To tell the truth it was pitch dark: it was all I could do to feel my way along the pavement. Close behind me—I was unable to guess how close—the shuffling footsteps of the old man followed, accompanied by loud sniffs and frequent mutterings, and involuntarily I quickened my pace. Fortunately my building was not far, though far enough for me to imagine I was being trailed, to what end, I did not dare to think, but it was with some relief that I dashed into the lobby. My relief was short-lived. The old fellow was still behind me, his viscid snufflings now echoing in the high stairwell. My heart started. The thing was, above all, not to look back, not to lose ground, I told myself, as I began to race up the steps, taking them now two and three at a time, too flurried to search for the light which had popped out, plunging us once more into almost palpable darkness. I hardly knew how I made it to the fourth floor, or with what trembling ham-handedness I fitted the key into the lock, my knees buckling, only to hear the clash of an apartment door down below.

Oblivious, he had gone to bed; and it was only after a moment's fraught realisation that I collapsed laughing onto mine. It had never occurred to me that the newspaper man and I shared a building. Yet a few minutes' reflection made it seem preordained.

I had never seen him under that roof before, but now as if some spell were broken he was everywhere, on the steps, in the hallway, in the corridor which led out back to the trash; I met him on my way to the trash, on my way upstairs, collecting letters from my box in the hall: a small, hunched, unobtrusive man, whose name, when I tried surreptitiously to read it on his own mailbox, was so worn and faded as to be illegible. But I recalled the landlady's bilious complaints, against that man, that old devil, Cacik, or Tzatzkes, whose disgusting personal habits she insisted on describing. I had never understood who it was she meant, and had even wondered sometimes whether he might be a figment of her proprietorial imagination, but I decided now that this must be the Cacik she so resented.

He did fit the part: was tattered, and malodorous, and carried with him always, like a permanent prosthesis, a small transistor radio on which he listened to the world news. In his ancient slippers with zips, whose disintegrating soles flapped under him, he shambled back and forth between the mailbox and his room on the third floor, for he lived, apparently, in constant expectation of a message, though from whom, and of what nature, I could not ascertain. His daily visits to the backyard puzzled me at first, until through my own observations and the landlady's garbled testimony I established that he was not taking out rubbish but bringing it in, for he was a champion of thrift and a natural searcher through dustbins. This was, I suppose, the least harmless of his preoccupations. His coat, in which by daylight one could detect the faint traces of a Burberry check, was one of the more mildly objectionable things about him, but it seemed to inspire the old aristocrat with a kind of shamanistic horror.

I tried to extract more information from her, but it was impossible to ask her questions: she simply did not answer them, she had her own agenda. She talked and I listened, picking up, amongst a bewildering plethora of facts about people I had never heard of, the disclosure that he had lived there in that flat for a long time, a very long time perhaps, that he had lived there for a very long time alone; that she couldn't remove him, much as she wanted to, because he lowered the tone of the whole building: he frightened potential residents away. Oh, do not ask her about that devil Cacik! It wouldn't be going too far to call him the bane of her life. A good apartment, too, a big one: she might get twice what he paid her for it now. Only last week she had sent her grandson up there to speak to him, but it was no use. Good heavens, the state of the place! He had barely been able to set foot inside the door.

So the litany continued; and when I pressed her further on the subject, it seemed only that she couldn't evict Cacik because she couldn't; she must be tormented by him because she must; that this was a state of affairs which had always existed, and must go on existing, for the simple reason that she could not now imagine any other.

But as for Cacik himself, he seemed quite content for matters to continue as they were, and for whatever standoff was rumbling between himself and his landlady to endure, if necessary, until death should end it. He had an air of obliviousness, and went about his daily activities with the serene attitude of a monk, for whom nothing short of earthquake or insurrection will disturb the even tenor of his devotions. Only once did I see him exchange words with her ladyship, and then he responded to her shrill red-faced hysteria with the mild contempt of a husband who has been through it all before: an alienated husband who sees no point in divorce, so long as he can slope off with a shrug of the shoulders, a muttered 'Silly old bat,' and shut the door on his den.

I knew better than to interfere between them or even to pass comment. The one time I did so, remarking in the gentlest of tones that he seemed an innocuous old gentleman, after all, I was blasted by such a storm of protest I feared I had lost my landlady's goodwill forever, and in fact it was some time before she deigned to speak to me again. Such an incorrigible gossip could not resist me for long, however; though I was now cast, despite my most strenuous attempts at neutrality, as a confirmed crony of Cacik.

A crony of Cacik's I was not: we had never spoken to each other, and for all my tourist's curiosity I had not obtained more than a glimpse into his dingy apartment, the door of which sometimes stood ajar when I passed by on the stairs. He must have been aware of my existence, though he didn't acknowledge it, and though I now nodded to him when I entered the Simon Peter Bar to find him sitting there in his usual place, he never returned my nod. Instead he looked at me fiercely for a moment, and, I thought, not approvingly, through his black beady eyes, and returned to his newspaper with an air of having been unnecessarily distracted.

This did not bother me, since I fully expected to be beneath his notice—I along with the rest of the human race. He was a vaga-bond emperor, a trashcan king, rigidly dedicated to his royal routines, from which long tradition would not allow him to deviate by one iota. Those around him, too, were drawn implicitly into the rhythm of his ceremonial, from the waiter who set down his glass of water before him to the landlady who, it seemed, existed solely to be his penitential scourge. I myself played no part in this ritual, except per-haps as one of the vassal host whose vices would one day earn them a rightful comeuppance.

It amused me to read these things into his appearance and demeanour, while hearing nothing from the man himself; but I didn't think I was wrong, though I may have been influenced by the general atmosphere of that decayed city, which had lain asleep on its history for so long, and which was being shaken awake so late and so inap-propriately into a world of decadence. I felt it in the solitary streets, where I walked pursued by ghosts on the edge of dusk, and in the high-ceilinged coffee-halls where the trapped echoes of a century ago still bounced, and my own voice sounded thin, light and unimport-ant. It was easy to imagine that he, the denizen for so many years of a place like this, should be possessed by secrets more ancient and earth-shattering than any I might discover, traveller, visitant, will-o'-the-wisp that I was.

Yet I was conscious of a certain romance in these musings. And if there was a threadbare regality about Cacik, the truth of the matter was he led a miserable, lonely existence. Nobody ever came to visit him; I never witnessed him in conversation. He descended twice a day to examine the contents of his mailbox with pathetic eagerness, so much so that on several occasions I inserted my own unwanted circulars for the sheer pleasure of seeing him gather them up. It was obvious that there was no one from whom he might expect a letter or message. Yet while he stirred neither hand nor foot to break the glass dome under which he lived isolated from the world, he was ready to welcome whatever the world chose to slip beneath it like billets-doux from a distant lover.

In the same way, he listened constantly to the radio, whose interminable drone must have filled, for him, the void of a too anni-hilating silence. I heard it sometimes in the small hours, the disem-bodied voices arguing back and forth from his room immediately under mine; for there was a late-night political discussion programme he never missed, and being a light sleeper, I never missed it either. Occasionally, waking to the sound of its measured question and answer, half-listening, half-dreaming (I never could quite make out the words), I thought I shared for a moment his peculiar nightlife, that in some preternatural manner I had become him. I was filled then with a sense of unfathomable sadness, an almost intolerable burden of despair.

How could I know that the force which drove him was not despair but uncontainable hope, a hope so huge it swept away all other considerations, was almost totally consumed by itself? That his life reflected one ruling philosophy, of expectation deferred, to which he retained a dogged faithfulness?

Be that as it may, I was losing sleep on account of his obsession, and the time was approaching when I must do something about it. A number of options lay before me: either to continue as I was, which was impossible, or to complain to the landlady, which would be sui-cidal for both Cacik and for me. A third option remained, one which hardly appealed: that was, of course, to tackle Cacik myself. I won-dered how on earth I should go about it. But I decided to honey the bitterness of the occasion, so that in some way it should be pleasurable to us both; and that if I was to be cast in the role of a crony of Cacik's, I should at least throw myself vigorously into the part.

Attack is the best method of defence. I knew there were few things Cacik longed for more than a letter, so I wrote him one, a proper letter sealed in an envelope, and left it for him in his cubby-hole; and I can honestly say that I have rarely experienced a greater feeling of well-being than when I saw him pick it up. I had no idea what he was expecting, and knew he was certain to be disappointed, but the moment of anticipation seemed to me to be worth that. His face literally sparkled. The letter read as follows:

Dear Mr. Cacik,

Since we are near neighbours, and since we have not yet had an opportunity to introduce ourselves, I would be delighted if you would have tea with me tomorrow at four o'clock. I look forward very much to making your acquaintance.

Yours sincerely,

I seriously doubted whether he would turn up. Having rearranged my meagre furniture as comfortably as possible, and raiding the nearby bakery for its excellent pastries, I was startled to hear a knock on the door at three minutes past four. He was there; he had combed his hair. He wore a patched black jacket in place of his Burberry coat. He resembled nothing more than a boy who has been summoned to a Sunday tea party and has done his very best to look respectable just after some rough-and-tumble in the playground. He apologised for being a few minutes late, but had paused to listen to the four o'clock news.

Indeed, the little transistor hung at the end of his arm, mercifully turned off now, but still available, I supposed, in case of any lull in the conversation. I invited him to be seated. In his dark clothes he had the air of someone visiting the bereaved household after a funeral, and the mountainous plate of pastries seemed thoroughly appropriate. I thought, He has not done this for a long time. And he suddenly appeared to me in an utterly different light, as one in whom the traces of a gentleman were still evident, who had had manners once, and could dredge up, even now, the gestures and etiquette of a social being: the required forms which had been stamped on his memory. But more than this, he seemed to me to be a gentle man, a naïve, sweet fellow, as if behind the fierce brushwood of his outer defences there lurked not a lion but a timorous mouse; a mouse decoyed by a monstrous appetite for pastries, all five of which he despatched without reprieve.

No doubt there was some sentimentality in my assessment. He had his boorish moments after all, as he questioned me without much

94

tact about my own lifestyle, and seemed to take it for granted that I was rich, I suppose because I was a foreigner. Then, too, it was hard to tell how much of his talk was overlarded with lies. He also boasted of being rich himself, very rich, if anyone cared to know it, and all his money was, he wouldn't say where; but he could put his hand on it when he needed it. As the afternoon progressed he seemed as if drunk on sugar. I plied him with plenty of tea, and listened attentively to the strange, disjointed comments and observations in which, after years without conversation, he expressed himself.

What can I recall of his ramblings now which would make any sense, which would create, in any meaningful way, a picture of Cacik? He was not what he appeared; he appeared as he really was. Such paradox is the only adequate means of describing him. He came through to me as an image broken in pieces which did not wholly and properly fit together: a man behind whom the possibility of another man always lurked, someone who might have lived a very different life. Perhaps it was true to say that this potential was the real Cacik, and the person before me, hollow, wasted as he was, had not led any life worth mentioning, for the sole reason that he was still waiting for it to begin.

This much was evident from the things he told me, as for example, that he always kept a packed suitcase sitting on the top of his wardrobe in case of emergency, because one never knew when one might have to travel on; and, examining my cheap tableware, that he had never bothered to acquire china, since plates were unnecessary and difficult to transport. I could only attempt to imagine how he dined. But eating, too, was a frivolous luxury, or so he implied as he swallowed another cake: a needless distraction from the main business of life, the next item of news which he always awaited.

It was this preoccupation with news which was his chief characteristic, but to attempt to draw him out on the subject was to miss utterly: he simply could not separate himself from it. He could not regard it with that detachment necessary for discussion. He fell silent when I mentioned the topics of the day, as though these were things too personal to be talked of. And yet he did tell me, with great feeling and nostalgia, of his father's habit of following events almost as though his life depended on them; a habit which, he supposed, had been influential, and which he might say he had inherited from him.

At this point he rose, and, brushing the crumbs of pastry from his best jacket, walked over somewhat awkwardly to the window. I watched him for some moments as he contemplated the view. Eventually he remarked that I had a better view than his; and he admitted that in all the many years he had lived here, he had never ventured up to the fourth floor, that it was to him in a sense a foreign country. He continued to look at the city for a minute in silence, scanning its rooftops as though really seeing them for the first time; and then, as if speaking to himself, he murmured: Once in a while it would be nice to hear some good news. He turned to me, his eyes shining. We interrupt this bulletin to announce the coming of the Messiah, he said, softly. Just once. We interrupt this bulletin to announce the coming of the Messiah.

I thought this would be an opportune moment to cut to the main business of the visit, though there seemed to be no easy way to do it; and reaching into my pocket I brought out the little plastic earphone I had purchased. In the gentlest of terms I explained that, while I had invited him up for tea mainly in order to make his acquaintance, I also had to confess an ulterior motive: that although I fully sympathised with his compulsive listening, it sometimes interfered with my sleep a bit; and that perhaps this simple device might help us both. He looked surprised, and a little taken aback, and came over to the table somewhat flustered. I hastened to show how it worked. There was fumbling as he attempted unsuccessfully to fit the plug into his rather large and misshapen ear, and awkwardness as I tried to assist him; we got there in the end, but it seemed that some ineffable moment had passed. I was aware of having missed an opportunity, and when he left soon afterwards I sensed that he, too, felt in some way cheated.

Nevertheless, I did congratulate myself on having broken the ice between us; and though we never properly conversed again, I felt myself admitted to his recognition as an honorary stranger. I was now worthy of acknowledgment, and received a nod of greeting when we passed in the hall or laid eyes on each other in the Simon Peter Bar—a major achievement, if you consider that even the proprietor did not merit such a token of friendship.

It was strange that by an almost intangible adjustment such as this I should begin to feel myself, for the first time, a genuine resident of that aged building and of Simon Peter Street itself, if not of that city in which I never thought my stay would be anything other than transient. The bonhomie was brief, however. Not long afterwards we lost our landlady; perhaps she turned apoplectic when she found me to be a true crony of Cacik's. I heard from her well-dressed grandson, who had taken to haunting the stairwell in vampire fashion, that she had had to be removed to a nursing home. The rest of the story might have been predicted. The morning came when, glancing into Cacik's cubbyhole, I saw there what I had never expected to see: an item of mail, a real letter for Cacik, perhaps the one he had always waited for. Or perhaps not, for an identical envelope sat in my own letter box, and, in fact, in the box of every resident: an unequivocal notice of eviction. The grandson's schemes had come to their fruition, and the old leviathan of a building, in which his grandmother had sat so stubbornly and for so long, was to be converted and sold off at last for a mountain of money.

We were all given three months' grace, the news being greeted by some with a resigned shrug of the shoulders, by others with loud and ineffectual complaints. I could not imagine how Cacik would react. Nor did I have a chance to question him. That same day I returned at noon to be asked if I knew 'What Cacik had done?' What Cacik had done was to scarper without paying his final month's rent. The packed suitcase had finally come in useful: he had left his keys in the lock and disappeared.

I was sorry, but not surprised. Sorry not to have had the chance of saying good-bye to him, not surprised that he had reacted quickly to a circumstance for which he had for so long held himself in readiness. He imagined it, perhaps, to be a piece of persecution directed solely at him, and did not realise that the rest of us were included. Touched by a barb of real or imagined danger, he had been stung into action, and had run for some place of safety, who knows where.

97

On my way upstairs I noticed that the key of his room was still sitting in the lock, and I was unable to resist the temptation to look in on the apartment to which no one, so far as I knew, had ever been admitted, and where even the grandson himself had not dared to enter. The door was unlocked, but when I tried to open it, it met with resistance and only gave way a few inches. I managed to slip through. The obstacle, I found, was a pile of newspapers: a monstrous pile, almost as high as myself, and only one of dozens which filled the room. The air was fetid: one seemed to breathe newsprint, along with other less salutary smells. The blinds were half-closed over the dirty windows, and the light was dim, but it was easy to see that the place had not been cleaned or decorated in years. Spare as it was, it was difficult to manoeuvre through the rubbish. The whole table was covered with the empty packages from which, no doubt, he had eaten his food direct. I hardly dared glance into the tiny bathroom, in which brown stains ran down the crumbling walls; and everywhere were the heaps of newspapers, on floors, on furniture, strewn on the bed itself: the sacred newspapers he was sworn to scrutinize, to save religiously and never to discard, for the sake of the small advertisement lurking somewhere, the one which announced the coming of the Messiah.

I stood in silence and took in the full enormity of that place, and it seemed to me that this was the true testament of Cacik's life, a life of such minimalism that these newspapers surely recorded its only landmarks, and to that effect may have been rightly treasured and preserved by him. I thought of him arriving here as a young man, fleeing from who knows what chaotic trauma, to crouch, to hide, to wait until it was safe; I thought of all the years he had remained here, holding his breath in fantastic expectation. In such an existence, one might feel justified in hoping for transformation through some cataclysmic and unearned event; one might well be sustained by such a vision. But the place which had sheltered him would give shelter no longer, soon that too would be nothing but a facade: the new city dancing in the old one's garments, the thin guise of history on a mansion of ignorant air.

Issachar

The same journeying of the ten Tribes into India, is confirmed by that which P. Malvenda reports, That Arsareth is that Promontory which is neare to Scythia, called by Pliny, Tabis, where America is parted from the Country of Anian by a narrow Sea; which also on that side parts China, or Tartary from America; so that there might be an easy passage for the ten Tribes through Arsareth into the Kingdoms of Anian, and Quivira, which in time might plant the new world, and firme land; which in bignesse equals Europe, Asia, and Africa put together; Alonsus Augustinianus counting from the shoare of the North Sea, from the Country of Labrador 3928 miles, and from Sur 3000 miles; but Gomaras counts from India by the South, and Sur, 9,300 miles; which space is bigge enough for the ten Tribes, that they may there spread in places hitherto unknowne.

Manasseh ben Israel, *The Hope of Israel*

Archaeological and anthropological research has not unearthed any skulls of ancient Hebrews in Palestine. However, even without hard evidence, it is impossible for us to conclude a common ancestry for today's Jews, given their wide diversity of type. Such variety can only have been introduced by racial admixture, and to such a degree that one may be tempted to remark that modern Jews are not really Jews at all in any definable sense.

Kugelmann, *An Anthropology of the Jews*

What became, then, of the ten lost tribes? They melted away and vanished, like snow in water.

Anonymous writer, 16th Century

From there I went south, and after a few months in the sun I fled north again and drifted through the hinterlands of various cities. I taught night classes, and in the holidays I travelled. I was drawn east on a misunderstanding and stayed there on a whim. The whim proved disastrous, and I returned with painful memories and a scalded heart.

From there I lose track of myself, there are so many journeys and so many ports of call. If I had kept a diary I could itemise them. But I kept nothing extraneous, and little by little, as I moved on, I parted with what I did have, so that the porter, picking up my small suitcase, would ask inevitably: Is this all your luggage?

Impossible to list now the waggons, trucks, cars and sleepers, the packets, vans, tugs and trailers in which I travelled. Incredible to think of the succession of hotels and hostels, garrets and basements which, however briefly, I called home. And yet, with an acuteness of memory which is as good as any diary, I remember all the details: the black stove in the corner of the cellar which I fed with sticks one winter; the telephone number which I memorised, shivering, in an effort to get to sleep. The cold companionship of moonlight in a bare attic. The sunlight coming through the plane tree in a certain park.

And I remember the people, the conversations: the series of faces which brushed by me and were gone. The pale face of the violinist playing on the street corner. The grin of the ticket collector on the downtown tram. A quarrel about politics, a reconciliation. A late night spent discussing the end of the world.

But from the stream of people, I sought out those who, for the purposes of a kind of research, I chose to identify among the lost: that hidden tribe of wanderers and strangers, aliens and misfits to which I too belonged.

How did we know each other? I cannot say for certain that we did. But there were occasions when our eyes met, isolated moments in conversation, when we instinctively recognised ourselves.

As for me, I moved on and moved on again, compiling my haphazard almanac, my heart scalded, reticent to excess, closing up like a sea urchin at the least intrusion. I know that people said of me that I was reserved, a good teacher, courteous and dignified and old-fashioned. I do not imagine, once I was gone, that I left the slightest impression.

That is how I wished myself to be. It is an advantage to an observer to be anonymous. It is good for a confidant to be discreet. And it is true that I did have this effect on people, that they considered me a natural confessor.

That certainly appeared to be the case with Genie, who sat at the back of my Wednesday evening class and whom I didn't even notice until the night she stayed behind, after all the others had gone, and waited deliberately to draw my attention. It was strange, that first encounter, and somehow uncanny, because she took me completely by surprise. I had thought I was alone in the room, and suddenly there she was, mundane and motionless as a piece of furniture.

Perhaps it was because of the dark northern winter in which we met that she always looked cold and always inadequately dressed. Perhaps that was why she had a habit of clutching herself in her own arms, as if she would roll up in a ball like a lost puppy. When I first saw her she was crouched on a chair in this way, so tightly folded that at first glance I thought she was a forgotten cardigan or a rucksack.

Then I exclaimed as she uncurled and came towards me in a slow, lazy way, looking up from under a cloud of tousled hair. Her eyes were bright green, like the luminous dial on an alarm clock. I smiled, flustered. I said: Oh, I didn't see you! You're—But I had forgotten who she was; in fact I had never known her name.

But it was not like Genie to offer explanations, and I could only assume she was one of those students who had missed the first and second class, and slipped in, later, without an introduction. All the same, I was vexed with myself for not having noticed her. She was, apart from her eyes, someone it might have been easy to overlook: bony and underfed, she wore the regulation jeans and sweater; her voice and accent were unexceptional. She might have been plucked from any one of the institutions I had worked at, with their endlessly renewed hordes of impressible students, though she was so very slight and ordinary as to be hardly there.

I don't remember what she said on that first meeting, apart from, I'm Genie, murmured with a mysterious half-smile. Perhaps she asked me something about the lesson; then she wandered out with her hands in her back pockets and her shoulders hunched, in the standard attitude of an adolescent.

She wasn't present at the next week's class, which annoyed me, and I made a mental note to have words with her. But thereafter, for a while, she proved elusive. I would catch sight of her sometimes, as I thought, disappearing down a corridor, or waiting in the cafeteria queue; and once, through the glass panel of a door, I saw her sitting with her feet up at the back of another class, her preternatural green eyes fixed unmistakably on me. But I never succeeded in accosting her. These glimpses of Genie became in some troubling way associated with the endless winter through which we were struggling: a ghost roaming the white bunker of the institute with its bright lights and basement windows piled with never-melting snow.

And then, one Wednesday, the class filed out and there she was, standing this time just at my elbow, clutching her books to her chest and chewing gum. I was startled to see her. I felt I must be stern. Genie, I said, you've missed class again. Do you really think there is any point in coming? But I haven't missed any classes, she said, and to prove it she leafed back through the register on my desk, which was passed round during the course of every lesson, and on which she was listed each time as present.

I was well aware that that could have been done by subterfuge. All the same, I was momentarily lost for words. She smiled, almost pityingly, and said: You didn't notice me, you see. It was as though she expected nothing better.

I apologised. Next time, I suggested, perhaps you should sit nearer the front of the class. But I felt awkward, and gathering up my things, vacated the room hastily, leaving her behind.

To my surprise she followed me to the cafeteria, which was nearly deserted. She said: Do you mind if I join you? I said, Not at all. We each helped ourselves to a mug of overstewed coffee and sat down together at one of the metal tables. Genie seemed suddenly shy. She plucked at the moth holes in her skinny-rib jumper. Under the bright lights of the cafeteria I was uncertain for a moment how old she really was. Her face had that worn look of the undernourished. She might have been thirty; she might have been still a child.

I asked her where she was from originally. She told me the name of a small town in the west. Her parents had split up years ago and since then she had lived in various places. She never saw her parents now. She had no brothers or sisters. She was a bit of a drifter, she said. I apologised again for failing to notice her in class, and began to assure her it wasn't like me at all, but she cut in almost impatiently. It wasn't my fault. I was a good teacher. That was why she always came to my classes. It wasn't my fault she made no impression on people.

I wouldn't say that, I answered. You must know you have the most amazing eyes. Oh, these, she responded, laughing. You shouldn't be taken in by these. Abruptly she bent down over the table, put a hand to her face and removed something. When she looked up at me again, one of her eyes was green and the other blue.

It was an unsettling moment. She looked stranger than ever, and for a split second I wished we were not quite so alone in the cafeteria. If the eye was a window on the personality there was something eerie about a person who could hide behind a coloured contact lens.

She removed the other lens, and when she looked at me again she seemed diminished somehow, as though she had taken on the dullness of her surroundings and was camouflaged. She was right: she was an easy person to overlook.

I had to admit that, even when I had got to know Genie as well as I ever did, even when I had come to regard her as a friend. For although we met and talked many times that winter, I never could remember what she looked like. As soon as we parted company I could no longer visualise her. I thought it was my fault, but I suppose she just had one of those instantly forgettable faces.

I would make a point of seeking her out in class, and for all my best intentions, fail to see her, though when I called her by name she was always there. Sometimes, if I strained hard, I would manage to conjure her, like a mirage sustained by psychic concentration. She used to tell me that the effort on her part was just as great, and that it was only by a pooling of both our forces that she succeeded in making herself manifest.

I dismissed that as nonsense, of course, though I had to admit there was a grain of truth in what she said. But Genie exaggerated her problem, it seemed to me. One day I thought she was really taking things too far. It was in the student café across the road from the institute, where we had taken to meeting on account of its mugs of frothy hot chocolate. Six inches of fresh snow had just fallen; the windows were steamed up, the place was crowded, and sitting hunched in the corner Genie confessed to me her true belief about herself. I laughed out loud. Her face remained impassive: she was quite serious. Prove it, I said. She replied quietly: Prove otherwise. Easily done, I said, and turned to accost the person nearest me. He happened to be an eighteen-stone rugby player in a ski jacket the size of Denmark, and when I asked him if he could see the girl with brown hair sitting at my table, he merely stared at me as if I were insane. Not like that, said Genie. You just watch. And she got up and walked over to the serving counter.

She didn't say anything. She just stood there, and when she had been ignored for a full couple of minutes she returned wearing a melancholy smile of triumph.

That doesn't prove anything, I argued, except that the service here is pretty poor. Besides, I added, you didn't ask for service.

Genie swallowed the remains of her chocolate. I didn't say I was inaudible, she answered. I said I was invisible.

I remained unconvinced, and the next day I attempted a little research of my own. I asked around casually among various people in the institute if they knew Genie. The response was depressingly inadequate. Most had never heard of her, and when I tried to describe her the picture I drew was so nondescript it might have been anyone, or no one. Some of those who shared her class remembered me calling her by name, but they couldn't for the life of them remember what she looked like. One boy said, nodding, Yes, he did have this image of a girl with green contact lenses, but he hadn't seen her now for quite a while. Genie had stopped wearing her contact lenses several weeks ago.

We met in the park, on a day of crisp snow and bright sunshine, and when I told her the result of my enquiries she smiled a little, shrugged her shoulders, as if she had expected nothing different. She kicked up a shower of snow with the toe of her boot. I don't know what to think, I said at last, and she replied lightly: Oh, don't think anything! It doesn't matter! It's like I said to you—*prove otherwise.*

We went walking, and looked at the ice sculptures, whose transparent solidity fascinated us. It was half-term holiday and there were a lot of children out. She began to talk of her own childhood, which had been unhappy: she had learned early not to draw attention to herself. Later she had discovered her natural gift. It was not one she was alone in possessing.

What do you mean? I asked. She looked at me in surprise. Everyone knows, she said. The world is full of invisible people. In fact there are more and more of them every year.

In that case, perhaps you would point them out to me, I said.

She made sure to do so on all our subsequent walks. As winter wore on we crossed and recrossed the snowbound city, identifying that race of the unseen which, to my considerable discomfiture, moved apparently amongst the crowds of people. Genie picked them out with an unerring eye; and yet, left to myself, I couldn't have told them apart from anyone else. It was hard for me to judge the truth of her story, since it was in the nature of invisible people that as soon as your attention had been drawn to them they could be seen, and once they had mingled with the crowd again, identifying them became impossible. A surprisingly large number of them were children.

But what struck me most was the way Genie moved, as if imperceptibly, among the masses, dodging this way and that with practised skill, never colliding, as I did, with the unseeing hordes. She might have been a sprite or a spirit, melting and emerging between bodies. Not once did I see them throw her a glance of recognition. Then again, they did not seem to acknowledge my existence either.

Of course, I never committed myself one way or the other. But I listened to her, and perhaps, after all, that was what she most wanted. She said that she feared sometimes she was becoming inaudible as well as invisible: so many people ignored her when she spoke these days. I laughed. It's a common problem! I told her. She smiled slightly when she answered: That's exactly what I mean.

One afternoon we returned to my basement flat and I cooked omelettes while she sat in front of the fire, drying the melted snow which had settled in her hair and examining my very few possessions. She sat so quietly I was afraid of losing sight of her, nervous that if I turned my back she might disappear. But when I came out with the omelettes she was still sitting there. She smiled at me. The light of the bar heater shone on her hair and turned it golden, and as I leaned close to her she gave off a scent of meltwater and fresh air. I thought then that she was quite beautiful, and wondered how it was possible for her to go unnoticed. But never since then have I been able to remember exactly how she appeared to me at that moment.

That night she confided in me how much more difficult it was becoming for her to make people see her, what hard work it was. She did not know why, but it seemed to her that the world was becoming more ignorant and inimical every day. She was not alone in feeling this; others like her were struggling too. Soon, so great was the effort of maintaining themselves, she was afraid they would give up completely and disappear.

It was strange to hear her say these things, and to smell her scent, and to feel the soft down covering her skin. Her physical presence was so real, I couldn't believe in such transience. After we kissed I asked her whether she didn't think I, too, was one like her. She shook her head. Oh, no, she said, that isn't your problem, even though you'd like to think it is. I was rather taken aback. What is my problem then? I asked her. She looked around the bare room. You want to go home, she answered, but there is no such place.

It was true: the term was drawing to a close, my position was only temporary, and soon I would have to think of moving on. As for Genie, her studies were always haphazard and desultory. If I was leaving the institute, so was she. I asked her how she would manage, where she would find work? She looked hardened and contemptuous for a moment. Oh, she had ways of managing! Invisibility wasn't without its benefits.

I did not like to ask more, but I thought of a number of instances of petty theft which had been reported lately around college. And if that was how Genie 'managed,' perhaps there was a certain justice in it.

She had never even been properly registered and had paid no fees. And I began to understand what kind of a life it was she led: a half-life, really, an unofficial existence, which when it was over would leave no trace behind. Sometimes she had money, sometimes she was out of luck, and lived in the sewers or out of cardboard boxes. I never did understand why she had come to learn from me, unless it was simply because she was cold, and wandered into my classroom one evening to escape the snow.

Now the snow was starting to melt, and rivulets of meltwater were running down the walls of my basement flat where, more often than not, Genie now stopped over. I decided that my next destination would be somewhere hot. I tried to persuade Genie to accompany me. She laughed and tossed her head. What makes you think for one single moment—? But she didn't complete her question. It's like I said, she continued. You are always trying to find a home.

I was hurt by this, and it seemed to me that I had compromised my policy of self-containment only to run up against someone even more fiercely self-contained. I saw that I had put myself at Genie's mercy and that she would now begin to play games with me, which she duly did. The next time I called for her in class she did not answer.

It was inevitable, perhaps: I had begun to care too much. While I was anxiously counting our remaining days, Genie had grown impatient and run off. And how do you look for someone who is invisible? I pursued her everywhere: in the student dives, in the cafeteria, all through the park and even in the corners of my own flat. I pounded across town with my eyes burning, willing her to appear. I thought I could summon her by the sheer power of sight. I failed, of course. An invisible person is not very different from anyone else who does not wish to be found.

My last class brought me a round of applause and a leaving gift from my pupils, suggesting that I was not as insignificant a teacher as I had supposed. The card was signed by everyone, except Genie.

Afterwards I sat alone in the cafeteria and stared at the card, and realised that I was already beginning to find it difficult to put faces to the signatures, I who had always prided myself on my good memory. Some had vanished completely; others were no more than a blurred image. I began to reflect then on the intangibility of people, and wondered if I had ever really known Genie. I looked up, and there Genie was.

She was sitting opposite me, watching me, with her elbows on the table, as though she had been settled there for some time. She was smiling her broken smile, and for a moment I was uncertain whether it was really her, or just a vision I had finally succeeded in conjuring. I had wanted to see her again so very much. Then she presented me with a small envelope.

This is my leaving present, she said.

I opened it. Inside there was a blurred snapshot.

I knew then that she had come to say good-bye, and nothing I could do would persuade her otherwise. I sat and looked at her, tried to memorise the way she looked just then: the hair, the shape of the face, the shape of the eyes, the set of the shoulders, the colour of her skin. It was impossible. She reached across the table, and I held the warm hand of someone who claimed she was invisible, and who was as real to me at that moment as my own body.

I closed my eyes and felt it, and when I opened them again Genie was gone.

Outside the snow was all but melted, the crocuses and daffodils were pushing through, and I packed my one suitcase and headed south again, back to the steam and heat and the lands with no winter. I had had enough of snow, I thought, to last me a lifetime, though I knew that twelve months later I would be missing it again.

In my pocket I carried a snapshot which I looked at sometimes: a blurred girl's face, it both was and was not Genie. Genie wasn't photogenic, she didn't have the kind of face you could easily pin down. In any case, it wasn't a talisman by which to remember her. I often think how, on my travels, I might have passed her a dozen times in the street and not known her by that photograph. Once or twice I thought I glimpsed her, in a passing car, swept away from me in a moving crowd. But the truth is Genie has vanished. I cannot remember what Genie looked like. It is only the feel of her hand that I remember.

Zebulun

Let us trace the journey of the Tribes from Media to Britain. Historians agree that within a century of their exile to Media the ten tribes escaped. From that time on they existed under various guises. To the ancient Greeks and Romans they were known as Goths, as Scythians, as Sakai, and as hordes invading and settling the shores of the Black Sea. From there they travelled north, into Western Europe and Scandinavia; and those Saxons who captured these isles from the ancient Britons were none other than Sac's Sons—the sons of Isaac.

Rev. John Austen, *Secrets of the Tribes*

On the other side of this river there dwell the tribes of Simeon, of Zebulun and of Asher. The extent of their land is twenty days' journey, and they have towns in the mountains. They are not under the rule of the Gentiles, but have a prince of their own, who is a wise man and a scholar of the Torah. It is said of them that they know nothing of the world at large, but live separately and at peace, praying always for the End of Days and the coming of the Messiah.

Eliezer ben Levi, *Travels to the Ten Lost Tribes*

Sonos Judios: We are Jews

Inscription in Spanish breviary, 19th Century

H e was a prince in his own palace. That was what I thought the first time I went to see him, in the old colonial-style mansion, deep in the heart of the garden district, where he lived. I stood at one end of the huge hall and he at the other. And he introduced himself rather ponderously, with a regal formality which could not fail to amuse.

Even then I knew better than to show it. There was something in his face which forbade all laughter, which even frowned on smiles, and I did not want to risk losing his regard before I had gained it. He had very large, very clear grey eyes, and when they fixed on me, even at a distance, I was subdued into a kind of obliging readiness to do his will.

I remained where I was and he came down the hall towards me, with his characteristic gliding walk, dressed in the blue tunic and trousers he always wore, and he held out his hand, which was unexpectedly cool. His face was unmarked, and it seemed to me even then, not entirely human. He had what I thought of, without prompting, as an unearthly beauty.

I had been told that he was difficult to be friends with, difficult to know. I have to say this was not my experience. There sprang up between us an almost immediate trust. And yet for all that we shared I cannot claim really to have known him, who did not more than partially know himself. There was always about him something unknowable.

Perhaps it was my status as perpetual foreigner which attracted him from the beginning, from that first walk around the garden during which he so endearingly held me by the hand, and won, I think, a part of my heart which had never yet been conquered, some tender place which until then I did not know I possessed. And what a paradise that garden was, with its vines and roses in the cool courtyard, the fountain which ran from the mouth of a stone fish, and the live gold ones swimming in the pool below; a place where it seemed anyone might have been happy, but where he, for such unaccountable reasons, was not. So that when he asked me to tell him about my travels it was with real interest, as one who not only shared my sense of displacement but who actually believed I might have journeyed all this way just to encounter him. And I could not help being filled, as he was, with a feeling that we had been meant for each other.

I think it was at this initial meeting that he confessed, quite frankly, that he was prepared to learn whatever I had to teach, but only on the condition that I was ready to learn from him, too. There must be no false hierarchy in the relationship. His imperious manner made me smile inwardly, but I agreed without hesitation. I said that I fully expected the arrangement to be reciprocal. I only hoped he did not expect me to refund my fee.

The solemnity with which he nodded approval on this made me think that he must have lived a life entirely without humour. That was when I began to feel truly sorry for him. The air of sadness which hung around him was almost palpable. When I held his hand it communicated itself with mournful, teasing insistence.

But he expected no sympathy. Before I left that day I was requested to sign a Draconian business contract. I went away feeling a little angry. The next time I saw him he was sucking up melted ice cream through a straw, in the huge upstairs room where he spent most of his hours because, apparently, the weather hardly ever suited him.

It was not a scene calculated to reawaken my more tender feelings. The windows were all closed and the room was unbearably stuffy. He sat at a low table at the far end, and I waded towards him through a sea of flung clothes and discarded objects, banging my knee against a prie-dieu. He watched me through one eye and said not a word. A maid in a black uniform was standing next to him with a tub under her arm, adding, at intervals, another scoop of ice cream to his bowl; and she, too, watched my approach as though I had just landed from a distant planet.

While I waited for him to acknowledge me I took in the full awfulness of that room, in which perhaps his whole life was contained, from the bottle he had sucked on as a baby to the shoes he had discarded last year, and in which the sheer squalor expressed so much that could not be said about his existence. Later he would tell me that the servants were forbidden to tidy anything, apparently because it was in his own interest, but this was one lesson he had never learned. In fact it had become a matter of principle to let the chaos accumulate. Nothing he had ever possessed had mattered to him one iota. He had paid a momentary attention to things and then thrown them down, and that was where they lay forever broken and finished with. But I was shocked to find other evidence of his strange detachment, the rotting food and soiled items scattered amongst the debris, to which he and even the servants themselves, from long custom, had become quite oblivious.

Yet it was my duty to ignore these things, to focus only on him, in whose curiously vacant face I could read nothing but ignorance, bewilderment, an appeal which did not know how to frame itself; whose large eye seemed to challenge me and then, coolly lowered, did not seem to care.

I remember I followed him down the long corridor topped with heavy cornices to the old brown verandah at the back of the house, a glassed-in verandah where they used to hang the washing but which became our place, with a chipped table and a couple of chairs, and a bit of a breeze which blew in the afternoons. He was like a long-term invalid leaving the sick room for the first time, cautious and careful of his lungs, covering himself up, though I knew there was nothing physically wrong with him. It was there that he described to me, piece by piece, his partial sense of who he really was: not this person he appeared to be, of course, but something quite other; and his absolute certainty that he did not belong in this place. It was not a matter for question, as I found out very quickly, but, so far as he was concerned, a rather mundane matter of fact, and the fundamental reason for his strangeness.

All this emerged somewhat haphazardly and without drama. In fact, for a long time he seemed more interested in talking about my past than about his own. I sensed from the beginning that he expected me to know instinctively what he himself was barely able to tell me, both from its being inexpressible and also from a kind of embarrassment. And the truth is that I did know, I did feel it, though I also could not put it into words. If I had attempted to do so I would have thought it ridiculous, and, as I soon discovered, that was his inhibition too.

Harsh experience had made him cautious, and he had good reason to be afraid of laughter. That was why he did not say a great deal. Perhaps even I listened with too much patience, for he would break off, on the edge of confessing something, and pay renewed attention to our game of chess; and a faint line of frustration would appear between his nearly invisible brows.

But I did not bother to protest my belief in a melancholy that was so obvious, nor could I deny that I was deeply affected by his alien state. At the end of our session I would let myself out of that house, which was always oddly deserted yet where one felt perpetually watched; I would be chilled to the bone, and it was not until I returned to the normality of the streets that I realised what kind of weird influence I had been under.

Occasionally, too, I would go in search of Mrs. Mendoza along numerous immaculate and empty passageways, finding her more by instinct than intention, for the house seemed endless, big as a ship and just as complicated, studded here and there with odd busts and religious paintings, like a gallery no one ever visited. I would find her tending her plants or arranging flowers, or looking businesslike behind a large desk, and always in a room I had never seen before:

some perfect room decorated in oyster pearl or forest green, with long windows reaching to the floor, and an air of timeless, undisturbed gentility.

She would smile at me sometimes and sometimes not, for she was not generally pleased to see me. She would make no enquiries, but wait for me to speak. For if she lived in the bow of the vessel, he was in the stern, and she did not particularly wish for news from there. I believe they met occasionally amidships, in the dark baronial dining room I had glimpsed once, hung with hunting regalia, but these encounters she kept to the minimum. They must have been awkward affairs. While I talked she half-listened, or perhaps did not listen at all, but kept her head cocked prettily and shuffled some papers; and afterwards she would repeat whatever she usually repeated, that Jacky was moody, that Jacky was difficult, that Jacky was always accustomed to be strange. Perhaps I too did not listen, or did not believe her, which was why we were doomed to replay, as though for the first time, the same unreal performance in so many different rooms.

I would walk away from those meetings angry and disturbed, disturbed at her detachment, angry at myself for failing once again to convey the seriousness of my concern. For it would be almost certain he was not eating again, or not getting out of bed, or on the other hand not sleeping, but sitting up all night staring at the moon. That is why they call it lunacy, the maid once had the insolence to tell me. He is not mad, I very sternly replied. She shrugged her shoulders. It did not matter to her whether he was mad or not; she had her own opinion. But she would pass me on the stairs sometimes, carrying a mess of slops, and when I asked to examine it she would answer: I am not supposed to talk to you about that. I became convinced there was some kind of conspiracy I was not allowed to enter, which prevented my ever truly helping him.

It was a matter of common knowledge, after all, on the street, in the neighbourhood, that that Jacky Mendoza who lived in the big house, the last of an old family who never showed his face, was touched—'touched,' as they called it—though touched by what, they could only speculate. Nor did I know what invisible wing had brushed him, though I might have guessed sometimes, on the nights we sat up gazing at the stars from the big window of his dressing room. Then the cold light, marking the hollows of his face, seemed to make him something ethereal: he would meditate on the planet lost in space, the people riding it, gaily almost, almost oblivious, ignorant of where they were speeding to. Their complacency struck him as nearly incredible. Clinging to the bars of his iron bed his knuckles were white, his expression a silent scream. He appeared to me then as one who might fly off, spinning, into the universe, from sheer inability to stand the pace, like a child flung off from a playground whirligig.

Perhaps it is moving too fast for you, I said. He agreed that he did seem to find it difficult, and that the air, too, did not breathe well for him; that the weather was always too warm and the atmosphere too dense, and the scent of some bush, growing in the garden, made him feel as if he would suffocate. Those times, also, when he rejected his meals, it seemed that all food sickened him; the thought of eating was utterly disgusting. Even when well, he could only take those slops and messes they boiled up for him in the kitchen, and they could think what they liked, but that was the nourishment which came most naturally—baby food, as the cook disapprovingly called it. But the reason he could not eat was that he was filled with something so uncontainable he was ready to choke on it: the terrible feeling he had always known and which he could only describe to me as homesickness.

But the doctor had been called in and had found nothing, except what he termed a slight neurasthenia. He recommended plenty of exercise. Then, there is nothing particular about him, nothing strange? I had asked once, thinking of some characteristic, a webbed foot or a second heart perhaps, to indicate his true nature. The doctor was brusque. He is perfectly normal, he said. Do not encourage him in his fantasies.

I did not need to encourage him, though I did listen when no one else would, and was torn by compassion at the things he told me. He showed me, too, the wounds the doctor had refused to see, the bruise of rough handling and the blush of heat, which filled me with fury, on his delicate skin. And yet I was obliged to silence by those other injuries, the self-inflicted slashes, the needle pricks, by means of which, he said, he experimented to discover what he was really made of.

I asked him once what he expected to find. Nothing, he replied with a sigh, and the disappointment of years was in his answer. These were, after all, old wounds, old scars. He had long since abandoned the search for practical evidence. His body was a trap without exit, his true identity a feeling, merely. And how could one prove the truth of feelings? From the day he first looked in the mirror and knew that the face he saw was not his, he had been engaged in an endless and futile struggle.

These were the secrets he chose to share with me. They filled our lessons and spilled over into the evenings. Often, at his own request, I would not leave at night, but would watch over him patiently until, suckling on his own little finger like a wizened teat, he fell asleep at last; and I would go wandering then through the silent house, its heavy sideboards laden with pale silver and its old mirrors shining with many moons. Room after room the furniture lurked in darkness, the monstrous sofas, the inlaid escritoires, the hideous porcelain stoves imported from a French château. I saw that all these ancient objects, this clutter of artwork to which he laid no claim, were as much a part of himself as his famed madness, that without them he would not be half of what he was, be it the buhl timepiece, the carved elephant's tusk, or the portrait in oils of his dead father, to whose Spanish features his own bore no resemblance.

But I would tire of exploring these things, whose tawdry weight began to bear me down, just as they did him, I supposed, without his even knowing. Time and again I escaped to the dark garden, where the sound of invisible water lured me on, and the scent of the flowers intensified in the tropical night; time and again I would bury my face in the heart of some alien bloom, as if to drink in the full quality of that perfume. I thought then that I would drown in pure distance, that I too might choke on this foreign air, having come so far from everything I once knew and being, now, so irrevocably a stranger.

I cannot even remember how long I stayed in that house, obliged by a rigorous and unfair contract, according to which I was made to sit for hours in an empty room, turning the pages of some book bound in patterned leather, the Confessions of St. Augustine, the Visions of the True Cross, the Life and Campaigns of Simón Bolívar, to be told at the end of half a day that Jacky was not available for lessons. I would emerge then, reeling, into the crashing heat of that latitude at that season, not knowing what to do with myself; angry, I would sit at a bar till evening and drink minerals. But the next day I would be back, slavishly dazzled by the white cruel house amongst its green lawns, asking after the health of Mr. Mendoza, and Jacky, who might be lying flat, or sitting up, or wheeling himself in a ridiculous wheelchair, would want me to read poetry to him all morning.

I would wonder then whether I was not the one being duped, a foolish victim of his whims and vagaries, and I would recall with a shudder the times I had listened reverently to his bizarre dreams which he mistook for memories: of falling, at tremendous speed, from a far point of light, or of nestling comfortably in some womb which was not his mother's, or of floating bodiless among the stars; all snatches, as he thought, of some other existence. These were, I considered, visions of which anyone might be capable, except that he had an unusually fluid mind. And then he would touch me with that light hand, and fix me with those eyes of indefinite depth, and I would be forced to draw back, instinctively, from a contact too uncanny.

I will never forget the night he insisted on taking me on his own tour of the house where for so long now he had remained a prisoner, and which he knew so intimately it was almost an extension of his own body; leading me into rooms I had never guessed existed, into whole wings I would not have suspected from the outside. Somewhere, in the far reaches of that strange palace, Mrs. Mendoza slept in a tall, gauzy bed, a blue nightlight beside her; and down in the depths of the servant quarters the silent, moustachioed butler and the sour maid lay ignorant of our nocturnal ramblings. In an unvisited library he showed me the case of dinosaur bones his father had collected, hidden beneath a piece of green felt, and for a long time he lingered over the fossils of ancient sea creatures whose vertebrae he traced with a spatulate finger. He opened books to display the rings of the Inferno and the far reaches of Heaven, and pointed out to me the pictures which most haunted him: those in which the clouds opened to reveal a pillar of fire, or people ran from before a deluge with the eyes of frightened animals.

As he glided next to me his pale, luminous face seemed to hover above the darkness of his body, like a small moon casting its faint radiance onto everything we saw, and I was conscious, at odd moments, of the powerful presence of something other, accompanying me through the river of dim rooms to the heart of the house. He would stop sometimes to rub his cheek against a velvet hanging, or to feel with his own hands the satin of some ancestral robe, and also to pick up, with a vague air of significance, a rosary of teeth which lay in a forgotten drawer of one of the upper chambers. It seemed to me then that he was touching for a moment the unremembered rituals of a lost age. But the moment passed, and we moved on to other items, other bric-à-brac.

Never did he pause so long as over a yellow globe of the world which sat on its side in one of the last lumber rooms. He seemed to recognise it as though from a great distance. Perhaps he had stood on tiptoe once, from some point in space, and seen it hanging like this in its full glory; or perhaps it was only in one of those dreams of his. But he examined it now, not on his own account, but because of me, and touching the wildest and remotest places with his finger he foretold that I would soon be there. Taking my hand he applied my own finger to the green jungles, to the vast deserts which lay in store for me, and I did not argue, because I feared he knew better than I did what the future held.

Then, turning, for the first time he embraced me, quite tightly and without words. His skin smelt sweet and so real, I could hardly believe he was anything other than the commonest, most tender flesh and blood. In fact I was certain of it. I knew then that he would never solve this mystery of his own identity, which was all he knew of himself. I had asked him to tell me once, if he was able, what if anything he wished to be. Something beautiful, he answered, Something loved. But you are loved, I had told him. You are beautiful.

I was mistaken however, or at least, it would have taken more than my love to save him. How can I ever forget the impression created by that last interview, when I stood on the green carpet at the feet of Mrs. Mendoza, whose hard hair was drawn back into a cage of iron, whose teeth showed slightly as I tried to explain, how hopelessly, the truth about herself and him? She was beyond my reach, she was an ice woman. Her scorn was palpable as I said the words: Your son believes that he is not human. Yet I thought I saw in her eyes a moment of real fear. Then she tossed back her head in a splendid laugh. But surely you do not listen to such nonsense! He is a child—he is only twelve years old. Of course he will soon grow out of these fantasies.

I think she was glad then that I was leaving, that if I had not left of my own volition she would have given me notice, removed my influence hastily from the boy. She did not wish to encourage his strange behaviour. In children, of course, we do not call it madness; but there was enough talk already, and from that time, I knew, she would keep the shutters closed on the windows of the Mendoza house.

Yes: I knew he would sit there now, in that catastrophic back room, which day by day he would be more constrained to. That no tutors or visitors would come. That eventually perhaps even the doctor would cease to attend him, or only a strange man from the hospital, bringing syringes, would plunge him deeper into the refuge of dreams. He would grow old; his body would age, but his face would always be that of an innocent boy. For that reason alone, those who glimpsed him would speculate about his weird origins. But the maid who attended him would know the truth. I hoped she would be kind, that she would talk to him sometimes; and that even if he never answered she would endeavour, once every so often, to make him smile.

Ephraim

We may conclude, then, as regards the Jewish nose, that it is more the Jewish nostril than the nose itself which goes to form the characteristic Jewish expression. Ripley agrees with Jacobs on this point, and concludes that next to the dark hair and eyes and a swarthy skin, the nostrils are the most distinctive feature among Jews. But if this were the chief criterion of the Jewish cast of countenance, then very few Jews would look like Jews, because the nostrility is mostly found among Jews and Christians who have arched noses, and this sort of nose is met with in less than fifteen per cent of Jews. Among Jews who have straight or concave noses the 'nostrility' is hardly ever seen.

Fishberg, *The Jewish Nose*

Let the British people become convinced that they are the descendants of the ten tribes, and it will put the question of our national precedence in a light which we have not yet known and will probably give an impetus to Bible study in this country that we have never yet seen.

Rev. John Austen, *Secrets of the Tribes*

I said however: Perhaps his longing is stronger than his grasp.

Maimonides, *The Guide to the Perplexed*

A slim volume, displayed in the window of a provincial bookshop, caught my eye: I thought the name of the author was familiar. It was familiar; it was the name of an old student of mine. Years before, when he used to come to me for lessons, he had talked at great length about his literary ambitions. He has published at last, I thought, and seized with curiosity, I hurried into the shop to examine it.

The encounter (the one between myself and the slim volume) seemed too bizarrely accidental. How very odd that I should catch sight of it here, in a provincial town, on my way out of the country, when I was leaving the continent for what might prove to be the last time? That I should even bother to glance in the bookshop window, that Georg's book should be so prominently displayed, an obscure title by an obscure author—it all seemed an impossible coincidence.

There was in my eyes something magical about it. For had he not promised me, when we last parted years ago, that by hook or by crook he would somehow get a copy of his book to me, that is, if he ever managed to publish one, which did not at that time seem at all likely? I had given him my first forwarding address, but since then had moved on so many times that we had inevitably lost touch with each other. Our correspondence had quickly petered out, which was a pity, because his letters, which he drafted and redrafted, were always gems of polished beauty.

I had travelled on, but I had never forgotten him. He remained as clear as a photograph in my memory: the long, dark, narrow, nervous face, the long and narrow, equally nervous hands; the habit of a half-smile which seemed directed cynically at himself, whenever he accused himself of grandiosity. He looked downcast often, often a little depressed, and never quite comfortable in his clothes, which were those of a bureaucrat, for he always came to see me straight from work; and he used to place one long foot across his bony knee and twist his shoelace around his index finger. Occasionally in the course of conversation he would glance up and throw me a smile of really wonderful warmth; and then he would jump up and pace about the room sometimes in a state of almost comical enthusiasm. He applied himself to his studies with the diligence of a schoolboy, and loped off down the darkened street at the end of our lesson with the stride of an undertaker.

He came to me at a time when I was endeavouring to persuade myself that here, in this particular town, I would be able to settle, that I wasn't, after all, the incorrigible nomad I had thought myself. I had lived there five months. It seemed a long spell, and the town was, I felt, as good as any other, perhaps a little better than most. It had what a town should have, it had a park and a museum, shops and offices, houses and gardens; it had people of all sorts; it had a fine transport system and a ready escape route into the nearby hills. Perhaps it was a little too tidy, a little too pleased with itself, but that was a feature which soothed rather than troubled me. I thought it quite possible I might remain there for years, even, in my wilder moments, for a lifetime.

As for Georg, I think we liked each other immediately. He had a dry, humorous way of talking about himself, and amused me, at our very first meeting, with a brisk account of his background, no holds barred. He came from a family of failed writers and small-time journalists, lawyers and professional procrastinators, would-be great people who were too clever for their own good; he had long since felt himself doomed to follow in the family footsteps. It was impossible, he told me, for anyone with his surname to succeed except in a small way, though their aspirations were always inversely proportional to their achievements. So it was that his grandfather had set out to become a newspaper magnate and ended up bankrupt with a failed gazette; his father was going to be the lord chief justice and got no farther than the county court; his uncle went off to be a famous actor, but if he had become an actor he was not famous, because they had never heard of him again. All his aunts had poems stashed among their underwear, but only one had experienced any success: she made a decent living writing verses for greeting cards.

I told him we must be relatives, for our surnames were similar and our families frighteningly so. He agreed that it was quite possible; after all, he added, we were all related one way or another. We even looked for physical resemblances: there were none, except for a small bump beside the left ear, which might have been something or nothing.

What was his own personal thwarted ambition? He worked as a pen pusher in the municipal offices, but while he was composing reports and answering letters he was dreaming of the great book he would one day finish. That is, he dreamed in his lunch hour, because the rest of the time he was much too busy to do so. The book, which was not exactly a work of fiction and not precisely a work of fact, had filled his thoughts for the last seven years, and earlier versions had been discarded in the seven years before that. The idea had been born in him when he was still a boy, and he had spent the whole of his adulthood pursuing it.

It was not so much that he wanted to be a writer, he explained to me, as that he so passionately wanted to write this book, this one book, after which there would probably be no other; since it was, in his mind, the book to end all books, the book to which there could be no adequate sequel.

That might have sounded a touch arrogant. One would have to witness the twisted half-smile with which he made this confession to appreciate its self-deprecating irony. There was no angle of bitter humour he had not taken on his own predicament, no bubble of corrosive laughter with which he did not burn out the arrogance of his own words.

Naturally, I asked him what this masterpiece was to be about. He grew coy, and wouldn't tell me; it was impossible to discuss until it was finished. Then, he assured me, he would talk about it until the cows came home, but while in progress it was a chick in the egg: disaster would result if the shell were broken.

Nor was he sanguine about the work soon hatching, for, while he lived in hope, he knew himself too well to expect much. It formed by atoms and increased by molecules; it lay under constant threat of vivisection. More often than not, come the end of the week, he would have less than he started with, and at the end of a month he might write off the entire month's effort; or worse still, he would spend the next month tweaking with tweezers and doing scalpel work before deciding to throw out the whole experiment, getting down, as he put it, to what was clean, pure, bald and uncomplicated.

It was his intense perfectionism which made the job so difficult. I could see that in the way he laid out his ruler, pen and notebook ready for our lesson, and by the immaculate homework, written in tiny neat letters, which he presented for my inspection. Dark circles beneath his eyes bore witness to long nights of labour. He winced at my corrections, and seemed to regard any blemish on his page with horror.

It wasn't that he wanted to be this way; he couldn't help it. Obsessive pernicketiness was in his genes. Nothing could be more inimical to the free spirit of creation (said Georg) than to live one's whole life in this cage of exactitude, where nothing was ever finished because it must be perfect, and even seemingly finished things proved imperfect and therefore unfinished.

He blamed a bourgeois education for creating the bands of iron in which he lived, and the town for its stultifying atmosphere that hampered any kind of independent thought. This town, with its parades and its rose gardens, its clean streets and hydropathic spa, where he had lived his whole life and which he couldn't escape, he held largely responsible for his problems. It was too safe, he said, dull beyond reckoning, and there was something vicious about it. I asked him what he meant, and he replied with a metaphor: they were currently cleaning the stone frontage of the town hall at great expense, but its corridors were running with cockroaches.

But why did he stay then? The town was like a web, it lured you in; you were held by invisible threads, fixed and paralysed. Not a year had gone by since he turned twenty, that he had not intended to leave, and not a year had gone by that something had not prevented him. One time it was a family matter, another time it was work. Once he had been presented with a diligence award, which seemed a perfect point at which to make his exit, but then he was promoted, of course, and it would have been madness to turn down such advancement.

It might be difficult for me to believe, he went on, but he was actually a model citizen. No one suspected him of leading a double life, his nocturnal scribbling was a total secret, and apart from a slightly embarrassing fondness for literature he was generally regarded as a good egg. Every Friday night he went to drink beer with the chaps from the office, and he carried off the performance in medal-winning style. You wouldn't have guessed he wasn't completely normal. In fact, he was sometimes afraid of it himself. The transformation was so insidious, he thought he lost sight occasionally of who he really was, and it was only the mass of manuscript sitting on his nightstand when he crawled home of an evening which served to remind him.

He made me smile with such stories. He was so modest, so polite, his own smile, with which he told them, was so gently satirical, it was difficult to know what to take seriously in his harassed existence. He made light of real problems and turned epics on imaginary ones, and with his cynical discourse on town hall affairs, succeeded in undermining any respect I might have had for that venerable institution. Bit by bit he made me hate the whole town with affection. Once he had told me that the air was stupefying, I could never breathe in quite the same way; and he never stopped asking me why I had come here and how long I intended to remain.

It was Georg who arrived for his lesson one evening bearing a mysterious box, which he slipped beneath his chair before beginning, and ignored with studious intention for the whole hour, only to reveal at last, with a flourish, a blue-and-white birthday cake. For as he told me, no citizen could keep secrets from the town hall. I think it was the only time in all those years my birthday had been celebrated. Then he brought from his pocket a small parcel, slightly crushed by his stoop, as were most things he carried: a book, naturally, for his passion for writing was only outstripped by his love of reading, and by his reverence for those dead poets who, as he shyly put it, still teach us somewhat how to live.

I don't know what I had done to deserve these attentions, nor how many times he promised to bring me something of his own to read, only to baulk at it on each occasion. I think he even brought a few pages of manuscript once or twice. It was as though he had a bomb in his briefcase. It distracted him painfully throughout the entire lesson, and at the end he ran home with it, like a whippet with his tail between his legs. I was rather relieved, for while I did not seriously doubt the existence of his magnum opus, it had, while it remained speculative, a Platonic quality which was quite compelling.

The irony was that Georg felt the same way. At least, looking back, it seems to me that the reason he could not finish his task was simply this: that any real book could never have had the perfection of the one existing solely in his own head. That one, up there in the ether of potential, was beyond his reach; if he could have touched, he would have sullied it.

But anyway it struck me that he had chosen the wrong course, that he shouldn't really ever have started writing. Seeing the way he sat, with the tips of his fingers delicately pressed together, I thought he should have been a craftsman of some kind, a worker in wood or metal, a potter perhaps: he had the hands for it and the precision. And how much happier he might have been, I told myself, to be making real things which could be touched and held, rather than burning his brain out with fantasies. When I suggested this to him he laughed for a full minute. Not, he explained, because I reject your idea, but because the notion that I have spent my whole life chasing the wrong grail appeals to my sense of comedy.

Obviously, it was far too late for Georg. I realised as much the day I came across him in the town park, a year or so after our first meeting, and very nearly failed to recognise him. He had missed a few weeks' lessons, first because of illness, then pressure of work, and in the interval his face had perceptibly changed, fallen, darkened. His hair looked grey in the watery spring light. I thought perhaps I had caught him out of context, which was true, because he was feeding the ducks with an expression of absolute absence. But when he saw me he lit up with that most friendly of smiles. No one could have looked more misplaced in that mundane park where even the trees grew according to municipal regulations. His tall, stooping figure, his long hands casting the bread, belonged to a mediaeval or a biblical scene. We spoke of his work, and he said that for fourteen nights he had barely slept, because he had been riding the wave of a fantastic inspiration. He had found the timbre of a true utterance. Never mind the fact that next week he might discard it all again. It was another step along the difficult way.

I realised then that he would never give up, that the face I saw now would change and change again under this impossible tension: another year on he would be unrecognisable. The hope that kept him going was consuming him physically bit by bit, yet at the same time his metaphysical presence grew more potent. I remembered that the prophets had often been artisans, after all, or petty officials; and it was surely possible that years of patient effort, and strong desire, and the lure of ambition, the dying and rising god, should turn the most hidebound of pedants into an artist.

I couldn't await the issue. I was already planning my departure, for just the same complex and arbitrary reasons that had led me to come here in the first place—money, terms of employment, itchy feet—but also because Georg, with his satirical insights, had undermined my comfort a piece at a time, and finally ended my brief love affair with straitlaced provincial towns, however prettily floral. I felt that I couldn't breathe, that my brain would atrophy and go numb if I stayed much longer; and I could not help but wonder if that was precisely what was happening to him.

So we made our farewell. I wished him good luck; he promised to send me his book. For a year or two he wrote me those immaculate letters which I valued all the more for knowing how long it took to compose them, how very many drafts; though as usual he had managed to miss the point, since it is the charm of letters to be vibrant and casual. Sometimes I would look for his work, half-idly, on the shelves of a bookshop, though I never expected to see it, and never did so until that day, however many years after, when it so fortuitously caught my eye.

I entered the shop; I picked up a copy. My first thought was that it was extremely slim for the work of half a lifetime. But perhaps I was not surprised, for brevity can be as demanding in its own way as length. The title was exactly what I had imagined. I was about to open it—no. I would reserve that for a private moment. I was amazed to find myself trembling and nervous, too full of expectations which I was afraid to dash. Let me just buy a copy, I told myself, let me just take one. I hardly noticed the man, the proprietor, standing at my elbow.

That is my nephew's book, he said.

I turned and looked at him. He was tall, elderly, slightly stooped: an unmistakable relative of Georg's, indeed he might have been Georg in later life; and he opened up his yellow set of teeth in an unlovely evocation of Georg's smile. It's an excellent book, he said, and well worth reading, though I couldn't claim to be an impartial judge, but I think I have a knowledge of literature, and this is real literature, you can take my word for it. He tapped the book with his finger several times. I said that I was quite sure of it, for I was a friend of Georg myself, and I knew he would never have published anything he was not happy with. The proprietor's face lit up as if for a jubilee. In that case, he said, you know the quality of what you are buying! And he proceeded to tell me about his special offer.

It seemed that he was, in short, that uncle of Georg's who had run off to join the theatre so long before, and who had gone into trade instead, first in theatrical costumes, then floristry, and then fancy goods; and who had reached the apogee of his achievements in this small shop, with its old-fashioned Linotype in the basement where he ran off a few limited editions. Having renewed contact with his family some years ago, it had been his privilege, when the right time came, and, naturally, sharing the risk with his nephew, to produce what no other publisher would venture, namely Georg's book, and to take on the whole burden of selling it by giving it pride of place in his window. I should count myself lucky, he added, in happening on this unique opportunity, for I wasn't likely to find it anywhere else.

I was surprised to hear that Georg had taken the step of publishing through the firm, so to speak. He must surely have realised that any venture which bore the family name lay under nine curses. I could only imagine what kind of desperation had driven him to it, and what kind of devious manipulation. I held the book in my hand: it was cheaply produced, a little amateurish, and I saw in my mind's eye at that moment the series of frantic letters now sitting in his uncle's drawer, in which he had vainly pleaded for the whole edition to be pulped.

But I was already cornered, and found myself obliged, for the sake of friendship, to take up the offer of two for the price of one, despite the fact that I had already shed the majority of my belongings with the intention of travelling light. When I protested that I was shortly leaving the country the old man piled on another three copies gratis, in order, he said, that I might spread the word.

So I stumbled out of the shop laden with fifteen slim volumes where I would far more happily have slipped away with one. Taken in bulk, the book seemed considerably less appetising. I stuffed the copies into my baggage as best I could, and two days later I sailed from that continent.

The first morning of the voyage, I went up on deck to sit in the early sunshine. The sight of the book had so far occasioned a feeling of nausea I couldn't overcome, and I had put off opening it hitherto. Now there was no more avoiding it. I extracted a copy from my knapsack, dumped the rest at my feet and began to read.

What a strange day that was, in which I read so assiduously while the boat ploughed its way, first under a rising noon and then towards a deepening sunset, while the colours changed around me and the air chilled, and I did not even eat or drink but read simply, until my mouth was dry and my eyes ached. What a strange day's work that was. When I looked up at last I was surprised to find myself alone, for all the other passengers had long since gone below and I sat in the glare of a bright floodlight, washed out, exhausted and feeling dutiful, and struggling under a fugitive disappointment: a sensation which flickered like moths in a night lamp, which fled and returned troublingly, banging its light wings against my heart.

I should not have been surprised, I suppose, to find the actuality failing my expectations, for what book, what mere combination of words could have lived up to the ineffable idea I had of it? It is after all the fate of most to fall short in expression, though we do try, though we do try hard. But I could only wish that my friend had withheld himself, and restrained whatever folly had driven him to publish what could never be perfected. I noted, too, that the book was still unfinished, that it was impossible to guess how it ever might be finished. Yet what I had from it was a sense no words can convey, which brought the tears to my eyes and made me ache with longing: a sense of his presence, of himself simply.

When all these feelings had run through me I realised I was cold, and that a large moon was hanging low over the horizon. I shivered and drew my coat around me; I closed the book. I picked up the bagful of books which lay at my feet. They were so heavy. What on earth was I to do with them? Distribute them, perhaps, among the other passengers? Or spread the word, as I had been exhorted, in a foreign land? It would not have been his wish. Even now I could see him, toiling over the new draft which would be perfect, which would express everything. And one by one I posted the volumes into the oceanic silence.

Manasseh

Too long have these things remained hidden from us: behold, the time has come for us to assert our place among the nations. For 'now we see as through a glass darkly; but then face to face.' We have been ignorant of our true origin; we cannot perceive our path through history, nor tell which of the peoples may be kin to us.

Rev. John Austen, *Secrets of the Tribes*

On the other hand, taking the totality of evidence into consideration; given the wide distribution of Jews throughout the world; given their very diversity of appearance, it may be suggested, without incurring too violent an accusation of fantasising, that we are in a sense all Jews.

Kugelmann, *An Anthropology of the Jews*

What ever it be it appears that this river is somewhere, and that part of the ten Tribes are hid there; and I may say with Moses, 'And the Lord cast them out of their land in anger, and in wrath; Secret things belong to the Lord our God.' For it is not known when they shall return to their Countrey; neither can it perfectly be shewed where they are, God suffering it, as it is said, 'I determined to cast them forth unto the ends of the earth, and to make their remembrance cease from among men.' As if he should say, I will cast them unto the furthest places of the world that none may remember them; and therefore they are truly in Scripture called imprisoned, and lost.

Manasseh ben Israel, *The Hope of Israel*

I am really like a lost sheep in the night and in the mountains, or like a sheep which is running after this sheep. To be so lost and not have the strength to regret it.

Franz Kafka

I had nothing but the clothes I stood up in; my luggage, which I had parted with to an officious stevedore, had somehow found its way onto the boat downriver. By the time we discovered the blunder it was too late. We were well on our way towards the interior, and all my possessions were headed for the open sea.

A flurry of panic and protestation, of claim and counterclaim, was followed by a spell of exhausted calm, and I settled down on deck to absorb at leisure, for the first time, the passing spectacle of my surroundings. The river was busy here, bristling with shanties, makeshift jetties and superannuated steamers, whose rusted flanks ploughed ponderously against the flow. It was an old river, heavy with dirt and silt, curling its way towards its somnolent delta. Watching those strenuous currents I thought of my small suitcase sailing one way and me the other, and I was annoyed at first, because when this trip was over I had intended to go home. Then it occurred to me that I did not particularly care. I thought that whatever happened, I would manage somehow, and that where I was going I would not be in need of much. In this state of euphoric indifference I lay back, closed my eyes and fell into a liberating slumber.

How can I give an account of that dream in which I floated, disembodied, through immeasurable swathes of space and time, in which I seemed almost to take leave of myself and become no one? When I awoke the view had already changed. It was late afternoon, the sun was casting long shadows across the deck and the banks on both sides were darkened by thick foliage. This was to be expected, for we were travelling in the direction of the river's youth, and its childhood was in the jungle. Still, I had not thought we would leave civilisation behind so soon. Strange cries vibrated in the distance and the water was a deep ochre. I sat up abruptly, maybe too abruptly, and my head spun. I saw then that my guide was sitting beside me.

He was seated cross-legged on the low bench, and smoking a long cheroot with elegant concentration. His gaze was fixed on the trees, whose impenetrable and suggestive blackness might have focused the most distracted of minds, and in his case seemed to have induced a kind of trance; on my moving, however, he turned to me with a slow smile. He watched in silence while I struggled with a momentary dizziness which sent the whole boat spinning, taking meanwhile a couple of leisurely puffs on his cigar.

You have slept a long time, he said. We are already quite some distance from the port. And he gestured to the jungle, as though he were in some way its magical progenitor, a stage manager responsible for an impressive change of scene. I nodded, pressing my head, and wondered once more about the wisdom of this nine days' journey up the river, in pursuit of something mythical and unverified, against all my most natural instincts; led by this negligent and laid-back guide. Because for the first time in years I was tired of travelling, and for the first time in years I was ready to return.

I thought that at last I was beginning to be cured of restlessness, though perhaps I was merely beginning to be cured of youth. What could be less appropriate, in that case, than to take a boat upriver, where all that was familiar fell behind us hour by hour, and hour by hour we travelled deeper into a strange country, a gradual and complete abandonment to the alien and the unknown?

But my guide had told me of a man out here, who had lived in isolation for many years, of whom they said he was the last of his tribe: the sole survivor of an ancient culture, a curiosity for miles around, who maintained his strange traditions, so they claimed, in defiance of surrounding customs, and whose name in the local language was something like 'Isidore,' which for some reason my guide translated as 'the Jew.'

But why do you call him that? I had wanted to know. He shrugged his shoulders. Nevertheless, he had told me, this was the general name for him, even as far as the delta, where reports had reached them up until recent years; though it was some time since any traveller had returned from the interior with news of him. But it was common knowledge that he lived there still, more than a week upstream and three days into the forest, and there we might find him, my guide said, if we wanted to.

As for your luggage, he now said, leaning back, I am not sure we can recover it. But you will not be in need of a great deal there. A guide is what you require, he declared, pointing to himself with considerable satisfaction, which in light of our progress so far I thought unjustified. And from what I could gather he had never even seen this Isidore, whose appearance, seemingly, varied according to report, and was sometimes tall, fearsome and hunterlike, and sometimes slight and delicate, like the lemur, darting among the shadows of the trees; and who could be affable, even talkative, prepared to tell the whole story of his life, and at other times morose and taciturn, receiving visitors with hostility. So that I did not know how we should find this chameleon, nor how we might approach him if we did; and my confidence in my guide was hardly increased, when, asked about these things, he merely spread his hands.

Day was descending into night: the sun was a red ball to the west and moment by moment the shadows lengthened. Fingers of blackness spread across the river. The air had its own peculiar smell, of dank weed and wetness and decay, and the boat, scented with rottenness, seemed dragging itself reluctantly against the current. The treetops screamed and flapped; and down in the undergrowth some creature of the mud slipped almost noiselessly into the water. Beyond all this lay the pall of a great stillness: night such as I had never known, solitude such as I had never experienced.

So with my eyes half-closed I lay back and imagined the story of this Isidore, inventing those details no one could remember. I thought that the tribe he belonged to must have reached here in a time before history, so long ago that no one could say when. They came from over the mountains, they were not natives. Though their ways were different, they had remained, and some of their customs had even been adopted, as for example the laws of cleanliness, the initiation of children and the rules of levirate marriage, whereby a man was duty bound to marry the widow of his dead brother. And for their own part they had learned to grow cassava, to follow the rituals of the forest and to speak with their ancestors; so that in time you could hardly distinguish them from their neighbours, except for certain incantations they babbled, and their insistence on resting every seventh day. But as the years passed their numbers grew fewer, their traditions melted away, and those that survived married among the locals, until eventually you would not have guessed that there had once been a wave of incomers, different in every respect from the people of the jungle. Only the odd anthropologist, sailing upriver a hundred years ago to observe their customs and measure their heads, might have theorised to the contrary, and declared with the fervour of a biblical upbringing that here were the remnants of a lost tribe, the distant descendants of scattered Israelites.

But as for Isidore, who was he, was he really the last of them? Did he still lurk in some remote spot, muttering the bits of childhood prayers he remembered, the sanctification of the Sabbath maybe, or the memorial for the dead? What did it profit him to preserve these things which were on the point of vanishing, whose meaning nobody knew and which would die with him?

These were the speculations which drifted through me as the light failed and a cloud of outsized mosquitoes gathered in the bright navigation lamp. Darkness fell like a curtain, behind which the monotonous chug-chugging of the boat was magnified, and all the sounds of the forest took on a supernatural quality. It seemed to me then that we were surrounded by ghosts, by watchful malevolent spirits who begrudged our coming. It was time to go below, but still we remained, possessed by the river's somnolence, my guide located by the glow of his cheroot, his breathing steady; he might have been asleep, except that the red point of light moved periodically back and forth. Once he called out laconically to the skipper, who did not reply, and who for all we knew had been spirited away, leaving the boat to take its own channel.

But tell me more about this Isidore, I said, addressing the darkness, and out of the darkness my guide began to speak. Really the truth about him wasn't known, there was so much that was merely anecdotal. But in the welter of contradictory reports there always remained this one consistency: the fact of his difference, without which no one would ever have noticed him. It was a remarkable characteristic amongst a people whose customs were strong, whose social condition relied on etiquette, and who had been known to cast out those who did not accord, whether physically or otherwise, with their own standard of normality. There were some who said he was indeed one of these outcasts. Yet despite all this he had survived, and survived moreover as an object of reverence, mixed in with a large amount of curiosity. It would be true to say that he was a kind of mascot, a talisman whom people touched in order to make contact with something troubling and magical, and at the same time a symbol of fear, a necessary and hated stranger.

So he moved from the fringes of one settlement to another; sometimes he was brought food, sometimes he was driven on; always he was alone. Those who had seen him said he appeared melancholy, that he sat in corners like an animal, and there were even some who claimed to have seen him weep. But there were others who had come across him in the forest, singing strange songs in a strange language. They said then that he must be happy enough. But they did not fail to mention that his eyes frightened them. An encounter with him was always something memorable.

When I heard this I thought it quite possible that the fear was in his eyes, that in fact his oddness came of being pursued. I wondered if he wasn't really unremarkable, bewildered perhaps by the treatment he received, and forced into strangeness by a people to whom whatever was different was by definition threatening.

And yet, on the other hand, it might be quite the opposite, my

149

guide said, and out of his invisibility I heard him yawn. He stood up then, and I saw the motion of his dark arm as he tossed his cigar butt into the river. Let's go below, he added. You'll be eaten alive. He led me down to the moist and airless cabin.

There I clambered into a narrow box bed, which, when I had closed myself in, resembled nothing more than a coffin. For a long time I lay open-eyed in the darkness, my ears pricked for the whine of a mosquito and hearing only a silence more disturbing, now that the engines had stopped. My head ached, I felt half-suffocated, I was both too hot and too cold. Somehow I fell asleep, and woke with a start, at an unknown hour of the night, to find myself covered in sweat.

That was the beginning of a fever which carried me upriver for an indefinite number of days, and which kept me pinned down in that unventilated cabin, tossing and turning, dreaming chaotic dreams through which I plunged and rose as if through water: endless exhausting dreams where I struggled through jungle towards a destination I could never reach. I lost track of the hours I lay listening to the thump of the engines and the rain drumming meticulously on the tin roof, to the calls of the skipper and the shrieking birds, all those repetitive and hateful noises. I thought the journey would go on forever, that this diabolical river would never end. I thought I would never emerge from its sweaty labyrinth.

And during all this I knew I was quite alone, which might have been frightening except for the calm presence of my guide, who sat by me when the mood took him, his elbows resting on his knees and his chin in his hands, observing my face with moderate concern; mopping my forehead from time to time and offering me water or a morsel of food. I woke from tortured sleep and was grateful to see his features, quietly nonchalant and invested with a dumb trust. I cannot remember what he said to me, though sometimes he spoke in a slow, soft voice, and the images from his talking must have mingled strangely with my dreams: the face of Isidore, Isidore as a bird, a bird-faced Isidore flying over the jungle.

But at last we had reached the end of our upstream journey, and emerging unsteadily onto the forward deck I discovered the boat's nose nudging the undergrowth, at the point where a winding path slipped off into the forest. The helmsman was pointing and saying something I could not understand. I was still very weak. The warm air drenched me and there was not a breath of wind. Perhaps we should turn back, I said. He will turn back, my guide answered. We will continue. Don't concern yourself. It is not much further.

And so I found myself stumbling after him, along the undulating and root-wound track, following him as if in a vivid dream, deeper and deeper into the heart of the forest. And that track, like the river, seemed to never end, but meandered its way amongst black pools and giant trees, past the smell of death and steaming marshes, dividing and dividing into a hundred routes. I thought I would faint from exhaustion, in that endless pursuit of my guide's retreating back. But I was obliged to cling dizzily to his footsteps, or else be abandoned in a hopeless maze.

I do not know how long we wandered in the jungle. Days, perhaps, chasing a flock of vague hunches and contradictory reports, baulked, disappointed, tricked, misled. So long as there was light, we travelled; when night fell we stayed close to the fire, surrounded by slithering and rustling darkness. It was on one of these nights, half-sleeping and half-awake, that my guide told me another version of Isidore: that he was not a native of the place at all, but a traveller from the outside world like us, who had wandered into the jungle and lost himself; and that throughout the years of his wandering he had parted with his identity piece by piece, until he was neither one thing nor another, too strange to be a native, too far gone, now, ever to return. And though by all evidence he did not wish to be found, my guide remained sanguine, was never put out, and, I felt increasingly, was not particularly bothered either. In fact it became clear to me that he would quite happily have looked for Isidore forever, without impatience and without urgency, at least so long as he had nothing better to do. He was a faithful guide, after all, for he was in my pay, and the guiding instinct was natural with him.

At last we came to a village in a clearing, where they had heard of Isidore, and some claimed even to have seen him, and where it was rumoured that he was in the vicinity. But by this time I was weary of rumours and sceptical of all sightings, and I did not believe he was within a hundred miles. In fact, there were moments when I had begun to doubt his existence. That night we stayed in a hut on the edge of the settlement, though whether as honoured visitors or quarantined outsiders I could not be certain. I lay on the earth floor drenched in sweat, for my fever had never completely gone and now it seemed to be returning with a vengeance. I told my guide I felt I could not go on. He was unperturbed; squatting beside me he smiled gently, showing his broken teeth, and said that he would go on alone to investigate the trail. I am sure we will find him this time, he promised me. I have a feeling he is not far from here. It was then that I told him of my own misgivings. For a while he did not answer. He was once more almost invisible in the darkness, though he now smoked one of the thin pipes popular amongst the natives, and he took a few pulls on this before he replied. So far as I am concerned, he said, it doesn't make much difference. That is why I have been happy to guide you, and more than happy to have come so far. Like you I am a natural traveller, and if I were not with you I would be crossing the continent with somebody else. You have lost your appetite for it, or you would remember that the journey is its own purpose. But since you are tired now, I will follow the trail to its end. And when I come back I will tell you the rest of the story.

Soon afterwards I fell asleep; and when I woke the next morning he was already gone, having risen early in pursuit of a new rumour. He left me my full share of the supplies, and I could only hope that they would be sufficient to see me through until his promised return.

But five days have passed, and he is not back yet, nor do the locals, with whom I communicate by signs, bring any news of him. Either he has met with some accident, which I think unlikely, or his ever-mutating quest has drawn him on, beyond all possibility of return. Whatever the truth of the matter I must acknowledge that I am thoroughly lost, for even if I could make myself understood to these people, I do not believe they would lead me back to the river. I wake sometimes to discover them looking in on me as if on some curiosity, a creature from another time and place. But they are not unfriendly; they even seem to regard me with a certain reverence, and though I don't even know what date it is, they have brought me two rushlights for the day of rest. I lie here in my hut; so far I am still too weak to move. I drift in and out of consciousness, and in certain clear moments it seems to me that I cannot be lost, since the whole world is mine to wander in, and really I need no guide except myself. At others I think that I have never been anywhere, but am lying in my own bed, having taken a few drops in alcohol of some hallucinatory substance. Or I could still be in one of the back rooms of Mr. Shatzenberg's shop, waiting for my father to finish his conversation. It seems astonishing to me then how a whole life can be condensed into a moment. I pitch and roll on the prow of a tall ship; I ask myself over and over: Am I lost or am I free? Am I lost or free? And all the people I have loved and known, Nikos, old Cacik, the lady on the train, Jacky Mendoza, babbling Professor G., vanishing Genie, Georg and his book, Esdras, Isidore; I summon and invoke them one by one, while deep in my pocket my hand closes around the lemur's foot.

Acknowledgments

The author wishes to acknowledge the following books and authors, from whom the material for the epigraphs in this novel has been either adapted or quoted:

The Jews, by Maurice Fishberg, Walter Scott Publishing, London, 1911, for material on the Jewish nose. The paragraph on 'nostrility' is a direct quotation.

The Hope of Israel, by Manasseh ben Israel, Amsterdam, 1652, edited by Lucien Wolf, Macmillan 1901.

The Lost Tribes of Israel, by Reader Harris, Robert Banks & Son, London, 1907, for material on the Israelite origin of the British.

The Heir of the World, by A.S., James Nisbet & Co., London, 1876.

The Diaries of Franz Kafka, edited by Max Brod, translated by J. Kresh and M. Greenberg, Penguin, 1978.

Some sections of this book have appeared previously in the following publications, which the author gratefully acknowledges:

Nemonymous Magazine, edited by D.F. Lewis

Mordecai's First Brush with Love, edited by Laura Phillips and Marion Baraitser, Loki Books

Maggid, edited by Michael Kramer

Zeek Magazine, fiction editor: Joshua Cohen

About the Author

Tamar Yellin

Tamar Yellin was born in the north of England. Her father was a third generation Jerusalemite and her mother the daughter of a Polish immigrant. She began writing fiction at an early age, and the creative tension between her Jewish heritage and her Yorkshire roots has informed much of her work. She received the Pusey and Ellerton Prize for biblical Hebrew from Oxford University, and has worked as a teacher and lecturer in Judaism. Her first novel, *The Genizah at the House of Shepher*, appeared from The Toby Press in 2005 and was awarded the Sami Rohr Prize, the Ribalow Prize and was shortlisted for the Wingate Prize. Her collection, *Kafka in Brontëland and Other Stories*, appeared from The Toby Press in 2006 and was awarded the Reform Judaism Prize, was a finalist for the Edge Hill Prize, and was longlisted for the Frank O'Connor International Short Story Award.

Tamar Yellin lives in Yorkshire.

She has a website at: www.tamaryellin.com.

The fonts used in this book are from the Garamond family

The Award-Winning Saga of One Jerusalem Family Stretching Over Four Generations and 145 Years

When a young woman discovers an ancient biblical
codex amidst her great-grandfather's papers, she embarks on a
remarkable journey into her family's history and heritage.

"Yellin's first novel is
impossible to put down...
Beauty, deep love, and a
timelessness will likely
make it a classic."
—*Booklist* (starred review)

"A fascinating, labyrinthine
journey, joined to the
modern-day suspense...
Cohesively combines the
epic and personal sense of
sorrow and nostalgia
rooted in home."
—*Kirkus Reviews*

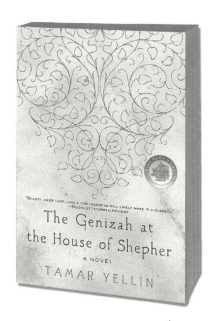

Winner of the Jewish Book Council's inaugural
Sami Rohr Prize for Jewish Literature

Winner of the *Hadassah Magazine*'s 2006 Ribalow Prize

Shortlisted for *Jewish Quarterly*'s Wingate Prize

Other works by Tamar Yellin
available from *The* Toby Press

The Genizah at the House of Shepher
Kafka in Brontëland and Other Stories

The Toby Press publishes fine writing,
available at leading bookstores everywhere. For more
information, please visit www.tobypress.com